BEHIND
THE
CABIN
DOOR

Deanna Ruttenberg

outskirts
press

Outskirts Press, Inc.
http://www.outskirtspress.com

Paperback ISBN: 978-1-9772-3379-0
Hardback ISBN: 978-1-9772-3465-0

Library of Congress Control Number: 2020918314

Outskirts Press and the "OP" logo are trademarks belonging to Outskirts Press, Inc.

PRINTED IN THE UNITED STATES OF AMERICA

DEDICATION

In memory of my mother, Irene.
Loved and missed.

and
To my friend, Annette Winter, whose contributions were
invaluable in completing this book.

ACKNOWLEDGEMENT

It is with sincere gratitude that I thank all the wonderful people whose help, love, and support encouraged me while writing my book.

Chapter 1

The only excitement I expected this summer was playing pranks with my friends, Pete and Seth. I had been away from our mountain retreat in North Carolina for the past two years due to my parents' divorce. I missed my twelfth birthday here, but things had finally settled down, and I'd have plenty of time to dream up the biggest prank of all. Little did I know what I'd be dragging them into.

I was on my way to meet them, drinking in the pine tree scent filling the fresh mountain air, when the strangest sight loomed into view. A tree house...yes, a flipping gigantic tree house, right in the middle of the forest, with a solitary cabin standing nearby behind a stone wall. I had to check it out, of course. Too tall to scale, but that didn't stop me. I managed to sneak in through a gate which surrounded the tree house. I climbed the ladder leaning against it only to find the door locked. So I descended the ladder and peered into the window of the cabin. I was staring at large unidentified boxes, guns, and loose piles of ammunition. Suddenly, I heard loud voices and footsteps. A voice in my head shouted, Run, Kate, but I didn't dare move. My hands were cold and clammy in a tight fist pressed against my thumping heart. I ran back to the tree house and hid beneath the mammoth tree that supported it. The voices and footsteps crept closer my way.

I stole a look around the tree. Two men came from inside the cabin where moments before I'd been peering through the window. The taller man dragged a short, tubby man by his shirt sleeve toward the tree house. He shook the man's arm.

He whispered, "I can't believe you came down."

"But, Nick—"

"You're the lookout guy, Joe. You're lucky Max hasn't come yet. If he caught you here instead of in that tree, you don't want to know what he'd do to you."

"I was thirsty," the short guy, Joe, said, his voice quivering. "I ran out of water. It's awful hot and humid out. Besides, I haven't seen Max around or anyone suspicious."

"Well, it's summertime now," said Nick. "There are more people about, so get back up there and keep watch. I have all these boxes inside to take care of. Get going before Max gets here."

I pulled back out of sight when the Joe guy headed toward me. He lugged his heavy body up to the tree house. The ladder groaned under his weight. Then the cabin door slammed. That must have been Nick going back inside. Silence.

It felt like hours hiding behind the tree, but really it was only about five minutes. The gate squeaked open and the sound of a car approached. Risking another peek, I saw a tall, thin man exiting a black van with dealer plates. The man stepped into clearer view. My eyes immediately fixed on his arms. I had never seen so many tattoos! It looked like he was wearing a shirt, but wasn't. His voice sounded gruff, and he had some kind of accent. Nick rushed out to meet him

"Good to see you, Max."

"Anything I need to know about? God, it's hot," said Max, and wiped his forehead with his shirt. He pointed to the tree house. "Lookout going okay?"

"Yeah."

"Good. Tell the guys not to make any plans. The last two shipments are coming in next week. And before you say anything, I'll tell you I'm not so happy about it either. But we're behind and can't risk being here much longer. If they give you any lip, reward them with enough cash. You know what to do. I already notified the guys at the cave."

My ears perked up hearing about a shipment and a cave. What kind of shipment? Where's the cave? Wait till I tell the twins. OMG. They were probably wondering where I was. I was late. We were supposed to meet up at their cabin. They were probably freaking out. I'm never late. All I'd wanted to do was check out that cool tree house, and now here I was spying on guys who gave me the shivers.

It was all so James Bond and exciting.

"Okay," said Max, "let's get to work. I want to be out of here before dark." He went inside the cabin. Nick began to unload the van.

Obviously, Max was the boss. I prayed they would finish quickly. My right leg was falling asleep. What I wouldn't do to stand on it right now, but couldn't risk getting up. As long as I kept still and quiet, no one would find me here. Suddenly, the cabin door slammed and hurried footsteps came my way. My heart slammed against my ribs. What if they know I'm here. I sunk lower onto the ground. My arms were wrapped around me, holding my shaking body. My head down. My eyes squeezed shut—waiting!

Any moment now, I expected a hand to reach out and grab me. But instead the footsteps stopped and someone banged on the tree house door above. I don't know how I held back from letting out a yelp, but I did. It took a couple of seconds to register they weren't after me.

Heavy footsteps climbed down from the tree house. I picked up bits and pieces of their conversation, something about a shipment again. By the time the men's footsteps faded, my shaking had subsided.

The cabin door slammed shut. I peered around the tree and ducked back fast when I saw Max approach in his van. I was more than ready to be out of there!

I listened for the sound of the van going through the gate before I chanced another look. All clear, no time to waste. I massaged the leg that had fallen asleep, half ran and half hopped toward the gate. I twisted the knob and nearly screamed in surprise when it fell off in my hand. I was trapped.

Doom flooded over me. I looked around wildly, then tried to reattach the knob—the action made the gate swing open. I hurried out, closing the gate gently behind me, then bolted to my bike. I nearly fell off trying to pedal while looking back to be sure no one was chasing me. No one was. Safe!

What was going on at that darn cabin? Shipments? Payments? I ruled out bird watching.

At the twins' cabin it looked like they had just arrived. Both their bikes were outside and Pete was hauling boxes from their parents' van into the house. Seth was probably inside. I got off my bike and crept up behind Pete and walked my fingers up the back of his neck.

"Aah," he yelped, slapping his hand on his neck. Then he swung around. I laughed as I wiggled my fingers at him.

Pete stood there staring at me, not uttering one word. "Earth to Pete," I said, waving my hand in front of him. "You okay?"

"Kate, you're back. Yuck, I thought there was something crawling on me." Then he yelled toward the house—"Hey, Seth, Kate's here and up to her old pranks."

I didn't remember him being this cute. And his voice was different, sort of huskier.

Seth came bounding out of the house. He did a double-take of me before dashing over.

He looked pretty different too. I skipped coming to our cabin last summer, so it had been a while since I last saw the twins. They'd really changed. Seth was wider instead of taller like Pete, and I almost didn't recognize him with those glasses he was wearing. Had I changed that much too?

Before anyone could say anything, I threw out my arms and we fist-punched each other like old times. Only this time they couldn't pull my ponytail because I'd cut my hair short. Gosh, it felt good to be back. It was tough being away from here last summer.

We laughed and talked all at once. We must have made a lot of noise because their dad yelled, "Hey, boys, what's going on out there?" He poked his head out the front door of their cabin. He was about to yell out something. But he saw me and said, "Welcome back, Kate. Good to see you. We missed you last summer. Okay, boys. Not too long since we have a lot of stuff to put away."

"Got it." Pete gave his dad a thumbs-up.

"Wearing glasses now, Seth," I said. "Glasses are in today. Those are cool." I took a step back and looked at him seriously. "Yep! Definitely cool."

"Really, I'm kinda still getting used to them. Just got them last week."

Only thirteen. "Now he can see what he's reading," teased Pete. He jumped back in time to avoid Seth's arm punch.

"Yeah, you wouldn't be so jolly if it was you. You lucked out with the good genes."

"For now anyway," said Pete. "You heard the doc. I could be a candidate down the road. What with both of our parents wearing glasses."

"Enough on glasses and genes," I cut in. "You won't believe where I just was."

I started telling them how I saw this tree house inside this walled property, and how I managed to get inside the grounds, and how there was a small stone cabin there, and how—

"Stop there," Seth interrupted. "You went inside? That was gutsy."

"Wait, you knew about it?" I said.

"Saw it last summer," Pete said. "That tree house on the other side of the wall looks cool. I'd kill for a closer look."

"Why didn't you tell me about it?"

"You weren't even here." Pete had a point. "Besides, we didn't check it out." Pete gave his brother the stink eye. "Seth didn't want to."

The big chicken—"Cluck, cluck," I said, knowing how Seth hated when I did that.

"I'm not a chicken. It's private property. As in 'Keep Out.' Pete could have gone without me. I wasn't stopping him."

Private property, my eye. Seth never liked to take chances.

"Right," said Pete, "a lot of fun that would have been. That high wall doesn't exactly say welcome. No way I could have done it by myself. Anyhow, the gate was locked. I couldn't have gotten in if I wanted to. How did you get inside, Kate? That's a pretty high wall to climb over. Even standing on your bike probably wouldn't have worked."

I crossed my arms, smiling proudly. "I walked in through the gate." They gaped at me. "Pretty brilliant, eh? If you had walked around the wall, you would have seen a wrought-iron gate big enough for a car to drive through. Next to that was a smaller gate."

"I did," said Pete. "But it was locked. And it opened just for you?" Suspicion was written all over his face.

"Yeah, I tried the knob and it opened easily. Guess bad guys can forget to lock their doors just like anybody else."

"What bad guys?" asked Seth in a raised voice.

That got their attention. "Listen up and I'll tell you."

The twins nodded their heads like, "Okay, then what?"

"I waited a few seconds before I looked. No one was around, so I went in and headed for the tree house."

"Golly, Kate," said Seth. "What if someone was there or a car came through the gate? That was really taking a chance, and you being all alone and that."

"No way was I leaving. It was my chance to snoop around and I took it. I climbed the ladder to the tree house. Can you believe it was locked? That ticked me off. Climbing all the way up there and not getting in. It's a miracle the knob didn't fall off from my pulling on it."

"Who locks a tree house?" asked Pete. "I never heard of that before."

"Yeah, that's what I thought. At least there was a window I could peek through."

"Whatcha see," asked Seth, "that had to be locked up."

"It was empty except for a chair and a telescope pointed towards the trails. At first I thought it was for watching birds, but now I don't think so."

"Why," asked Pete.

"I checked out the cabin after climbing down and peered through the window. I had to shield my eyes from the sun, but I could see in. There were boxes covered with blankets sitting in piles on the floor. A box of ammunition sat on top of one of the boxes."

"Ammo?!" Seth shuddered.

"Yep. On another, I saw some guns, and I'm not talking rifles for hunting. These were handguns. For *killlliiing*," I said in a spooky voice, pointing my hand at them like a gun.

The twins jumped backward. I laughed. A lot of people went hunting up here, so guns weren't really that weird to see. We all knew that. In all truth guns did sort of freak me out—but I wouldn't admit this to the twins.

"What happened next?" asked Pete, hanging on my every word.

"Well, loud voices sent me scrambling back to the tree house, and I hid behind the mammoth tree again."

I told the twins about Max, Nick, and Joe, about the shipment—whatever that was—and about the mention of a cave.

"How awesome is that?" I asked. "I mean, a cave? Caves equal adventure, always. Where do you think it is? We totally have to check that out."

"We?" asked Seth.

I sighed. I could see that checking out the cave of a suspicious group wasn't their cup of tea, which was so wrong. I mean, the twins wanted to be adventure writers. How could they do that if they didn't get over walls or through gates or explore caves? Adventure was throwing itself at us, and they wanted to hide in their house.

"Well, you guys always fantasize about adventures. You have to live them to become the great writers you want to be."

"And you fantasize about adventures when there aren't any," Seth said. "So some guys have a telescope and are expecting a shipment, so what? It's probably furniture or something for their cabin." He crossed his arms. "You probably just made it all up. You're saying all this just to scare me."

I knew it wasn't going be easy to get the twins to go back there with me if they knew how frightened I'd been. So, I'd have to leave that part out. It was going to take some convincing to get Seth to go along with this. He was always the last to give in.

I needed the help of the twins with me on this. Too risky and no fun to do alone. "Pete," I said, "trust me, there's a cave and it'll be cool. Let's go find it. You believe me, don't you?"

I held my breath waiting for Pete's answer.

Finally, he looked at me.

Chapter 1

The instant Pete smiled, I knew I had him. "I believe you," he said. "You're really brave."

Bingo!

Seth turned away from me, but not before I saw him silently parrot the words "you're really brave," at his brother and roll his eyes. This eye rolling was new to me. Maybe that's why he needed glasses.

"Back off," said Pete, punching his brother on the arm.

What's going on? Boy, the twins were sure acting weird. Or was this just being a teenager.

"So I was thinking," I continued, choosing to ignore them. "I'm not sure what's going on. But this would make a great summer adventure." I wanted to jump up and down with excitement. But the look on Seth's face held me back. The cave fascinated me. I thought back to all the summers coming here. Never saw a cave. Never even thought about one. Where was this cave? I couldn't wait to get started.

"Again with the we," said Seth, interrupting my thoughts. "Our past adventures were never this dangerous."

"No," I said. "They were silly, stupid little adventures. Now we're teenagers ready for something more exciting. Certainly we can spy on them from a distance. What's dangerous about doing that?" I looked at Seth. He hadn't changed. He took forever to give in to the silly adventures we did other summers. Seth liked to read about adventure in a book, period. Real life is dangerous.

Pete let out a loud sigh. "So it's a little risky, but this would be a real adventure. What a book it would make."

"We should go to the sheriff," said Seth, arms crossed, standing his ground. "There won't be a book if something happens to us."

"Oh, Seth," I said. "That's the whole point. We need some proof that they're doing something wrong so we can take this to the sheriff. No use going before we have proof. We need to spy on them and keep a record of what we see." How could he not see that?

"We could write this into the book..." Pete began.

"You could," I agreed excitedly.

"And the book could make us famous..." Pete went on.

"It could!" I said again. My eyes stayed fixed on Seth. He always talked about their writing a book together. Opportunity was looking him in the face. Open your eyes, Seth.

"You'd like that," said Pete. "Instead of fantasizing about adventures, we'd really be in one. Maybe we should."

"Not so fast," said Seth. "We gotta think about this. What if they catch us? It's too dangerous."

"I know I'm right, about going to the sheriff."

Now it was my turn to roll my eyes. "But we don't have

any evidence," I insisted. "No one is going to listen to us without evidence."

"I don't know," said Seth, his voice tentative and weak.

"It'll be fine," I said. "We're just gonna check the place out when they're not there. What's dangerous about that? Unless you're afraid…" And before I spoke another word, Pete cut in.

"We're not afraid. Come on, Seth, you're cool with this, right? A writer needs to be curious."

"Of course I'm curious. But not with this. No way," said Seth. "You're crazy to do this. You too, Kate. How can you even think of going back there after what happened? What if they had discovered you?"

"Well, they didn't," I said. "This can be exciting, guys. What an exciting adventure to tell your friends back home, plus the exciting book it could make. Look, we'll stake out the place for a while, see when they come and go at the cabin. Then we'll know when it's safe. We can also try to find the cave."

"Why are we even talking about this?" asked Seth. "Look at all these boxes. We need to finish getting moved in."

Seth hadn't changed much. He still changed the subject when he didn't want to talk about something. I would have thought he'd have grown up a bit.

"Look," said Pete, eyeing the boxes on the lawn. "We do have to finish unpacking. Can you come over this afternoon? We can talk about it more then."

Good old Pete. Always trying to avoid a fight, siding with his brother.

"Sorry, no can do," I said. "After lunch I'm going into town with Dad and Lily to pick up my birthday cake for the July Fourth celebration and my party. My thirteenth birthday. Yeah! I'm gonna be thirteen like you guys." I punched my fists up into the air and fist-punched Seth and Pete.

"Lily? Not the one and only Lily?" asked Pete.

He knew I hated my dad's editor. How could I not hate my dad's editor. She was so beautiful she made me sick.

"Yes, *the* Lily. She was supposed to be gone by the time I got here, but my mom had a business trip come up, so I'm here earlier than Dad expected. I'm sure Lily's as thrilled at my being here as I am seeing her. Maybe even as surprised. I know I was. Don't think my mom knew she'd be here either. She would have said something. Dad had conveniently forgotten to mention it. He just sloughed it off when I said something. Whatever. She's here working with him on his new book and should be gone in a few days—goodbye, good riddance."

"I'm looking forward to your party this year," said Pete. "It wasn't the same last year without you. We missed you, and celebrating your birthday."

"You mean you missed her yummy birthday cake," said Seth.

Not like I missed it. Being away last summer was tough. Of course my mom celebrated with me. We went to my favorite restaurant, where the waiter brought out a cupcake with a candle on it for dessert. Everyone sang Happy Birthday. Not the same with my dad not there.

"Yeah, that too," said Pete. Then he gave Seth one of those looks again, like a punch was coming, but just not right now. Weird. But I guess a lot can change between brothers in a year and a half. Maybe they just weren't the tight pals they used to be.

Back at the cabin, I found my dad outside reading. "Where's Lily?" I asked, hoping he'd say she'd gone back to Manhattan.

No such luck.

"Said she had an errand to run. She's picking up some sandwiches on the way back for lunch. Should be back anytime now."

"Dad, wait till you see the twins. I just left their cabin. Gosh, have they changed. I almost didn't recognize Seth and..."

"Kate, please, not now. I'm right in the middle of some-thing important and don't want to lose my train of thought. Surely this can wait till I come inside." Then he went back to his reading.

"Sure, Dad." Boy, do I miss my mom.

When I was upstairs, I ventured a peek inside the guest room. Lily's room for now. As a kid I was lectured about privacy, but this was Lily. My curiosity level was in high gear.

Inside the room, I noticed a piece of paper on the floor. It had a bunch of numbers on it. Probably inventory from the publishing house. Lily must have dropped it by mis-take. I wondered if my dad's books were in those numbers. He must sell a lot for his editor to come work with him away from big fancy New York.

I was snooping on, about to open a bureau drawer, when my ears alerted me that I was about to have company.

I bolted out of the room.

If the guest room wasn't behind the staircase, Lily would have seen me for sure.

I quickly snuck into the hall bathroom and flushed the toilet, making a whole lot of noise as I turned on the faucet, and then opened the door so that she'd think I'd been in the bathroom. I shouldn't have bothered. Lily had already gone inside her room and closed the door by the time I got out.

After lunch we headed to Asheville. I loved Asheville, a lot livelier than Lake Lure and only about a half hour from our cabin. But as we pulled into town, my dad suggested that while he ran some errands and picked up my birthday cake, I should go with Lily to see the new antique shop that opened up last year.

"My grandmother," piped in Lily, "introduced me to antiquing. It wasn't long before I became hooked."

This sounded like something that had been "orchestrated" earlier.

"Sure, Dad." See, I had no plans to stay with Lily. I'd ditch her and wander around town on my own, thank you very much.

My dad dropped us off at the antique shop. He'd be back soon to pick us up.

This shop used to be an art and shell museum. Now tables were spaced far apart so that people would not disturb the antique lamps displayed on them. No chance of knocking anything off these tables. I remembered doing that when it was still a shell shop. But here there was plenty of space to roam around. My mouth opened and my eyes blinked at the collection of antiques inside. I'd never seen anything like this before here. The shelves along the walls were filled with glassware, pottery, jewelry, art, iron work, and furniture. Only a few pieces were on each shelf. A big sign advertised that they did restoration work at a shop in Lake Lure. I recognized the street. Not too far from where our cabin was located.

"Quite a shop," said Lily. "I could spend all day here."

She must have seen the expression on my face because she laughed.

"Don't worry, Kate. We won't stay long. I'm going to inquire about the trunk I saw in the window and shop around a little before making a final decision. Since we're here, we might as well."

"Right," I said, and turned away with my antennae steering me in the direction of the jewelry.

I had never seen so many rings, bracelets, and necklaces. It didn't take long for me to stop edging toward the door for a getaway and start decorating my fingers and arms and neck with jewelry. I spotted a long antique mirror, and moved over to give myself a fancy twirl. I looked like a movie star.

But mid-twirl, I came face-to-face with Lily.

Shoot. How long has she been standing there?

"Ready?" she asked. "Your dad called and will be here shortly. I'm just waiting for someone to come out and get my trunk. I noticed a dent on one side, so they're going to restore it for me. Then, they'll ship it directly to my apartment in New York. I'll meet you up front."

I don't know what came over me. I squeezed and squeezed the jewelry as I dropped it back into the baskets. If I thought that would make me feel better, it didn't. The only thing it did was hurt my hands. I was afraid to look and see if I broke anything. As I turned away from the counter, I saw a huge wooden horse across the way. I imagined it coming to life, and I could get on and ride off. Instead, I looked for Lily.

A man stepped out from the back room heading our way. Lily had a paper in her hand and held it out to the man. "This is the shipping information you'll need," she said.

I couldn't hear what she said once she leaned down and pointed to the trunk. I'd never seen a trunk with so many labels. It looked decorative.

When I got a good look at the man, I did a double-take at who she was talking to. My jaw dropped. The man carrying away Lily's trunk was Joe from the tree house.

Chapter 3

We had dinner in Asheville and afterward I raced upstairs and texted the twins with my big news. For sure this would convince them that something was going on. They didn't text me back right away. Probably watching a movie; otherwise, I'm sure they would have answered me.

The following morning still no text, so I biked to the twins' house and heard blasting music. Bass rocking the ground out here. No way would they keep it that loud around their parents. Besides, the van was gone. Definitely alone.

I knocked and rang the doorbell. No one answered. Big surprise. Even I couldn't hear the bell chiming.

Then I stepped back and saw their window wide open. I yelled up to them. No one looked out. I checked in the back, but they weren't there. I tapped that doorbell a few more times. "C'mon, guys, open up." Nothing. That's it. If I tapped that bell again, I'd break it. It wasn't safe to throw pebbles at their open window. What if one of them poked his head out and got it right in the eye? That happened to a kid in my class back home, only it was a pellet from a BB gun. He almost lost sight in that eye.

Time for plan B. The oak tree in front of the twins' window. It had been a couple of years since I climbed this tree, or any other tree for that matter. Would the branch still hold me? Sure, I told myself. I'm not that much heavier. I zipped up the trunk and eased myself onto the branch.

It wasn't long before the trouble started. The branch creaked with my every movement. This wasn't good. I froze on the spot.

"Pete, Seth," I hollered. "Look out your window." But I was competing with Seth singing at the top of his lungs. It took five yells before he poked his head out.

"What are you doing out there?" said Seth. "That branch won't hold you. We got a rope downstairs. Hold on, I'll get Pete," he yelled, and dashed away.

I clutched the branch. I thought for sure that it would break from my trembling.

Pete and Seth returned with a heavy rope. "Tie this around you and go real slow," said Pete. "We've got the other end, and it's also tied to our bed."

Pete pitched the rope out to me so fast that I almost fell off the branch catching it. No wonder he was the pitcher for his baseball team back home. In slow motion, I tied the rope around my waist. Then I slithered along like a snake. With each creak my heart beat faster. The twins held tight to the other end as I crawled onto their roof. They pulled me inside their room. I collapsed on the floor shaking.

"You crazy?" yelled Seth. "Why didn't you ring the doorbell like normal people do?"

"I did, but you didn't answer," I said, annoyed. "And look what that rope did to my hands." I held them up. Boy, were they sore. Red too.

"Stop yelling at her," said Pete. "You okay?" When he realized he held my hand, he quickly jerked it away. "See, Seth's right, Kate. You could have gotten killed. We can't even climb that tree anymore. Dad's having someone come out next week to look at it."

That was the second time since I'd been back that Pete blushed. I turned away and mumbled something like, "Yeah, you're right."

"It's a good thing we had that rope," said Seth. "Dad usually keeps it in his van."

"Yeah, thanks, guys. But I wish I'd known about the tree before I climbed it." What else haven't you told me?

"So what's the rush?" said Seth. "I thought you were coming over late afternoon. I just finished breakfast. We woke up late today. You're lucky I'm a fast eater and was up here. Pete was still downstairs. He didn't tell me you were coming over earlier."

"Why would you even say that?" said Pete, grimacing. "You know I didn't know." He shook his head and turned away.

Boy, is he mad. Things seemed different this year.

"Just asked," said Seth with a satisfied look on his face.

"C'mon, guys, stop bickering. The reason I came early is I couldn't wait to share my news. I had texted you last night. Where were you?"

"We watched a great movie," said Pete. "Never heard the ping. So what's the news?"

"Listen up. Guess who I saw working in the antique shop yesterday?"

"I'll bite," said Pete, looking somewhat curious. I was glad Pete had calmed down. He never stayed mad too long. I doubt anyone would say that about me.

"Okay," said Seth, rolling his eyes again. His new thing, I guessed. He didn't look too curious. "I'll bite too," he said, surprising me.

"Joe from the tree house," I yelled out. "I almost freaked out, but there he was. Lily had bought a trunk. It had a dent, so they called a guy to come and get it to send to their restoration shop here in Lake Lure. You know that shop downtown? Well, it was Joe from the tree house who came out to get it. What do you think is going on? We have to investigate this. Oh, what an adventure this could be." Scaredy Seth was getting a cranky look. "We'd be real careful of course."

"So he's got a job at the antique shop," said Seth. "Lots of people have more than one job. The dude probably needs the money."

"Maybe," I said. I knew Seth could be right since a lot of people came to Lake Lure looking for summer jobs, especially since the movie *Dirty Dancing* was filmed here. It was an older movie that still rocked with us kids. But I knew an opportunity when I saw one and suggested we snoop around the grounds and the antique and restoration shop. "We'd all be together," I said, "and we'd watch out for each other. What if we found something going on that's illegal? Wow, what a story for the kids back home."

"We'd have to be sure no one's around," said Pete.

"Of course," I agreed.

"Those guys could be dangerous if they found us snooping around," piped in Seth.

"They're not going to find us," I said, giving Seth my best reassuring smile.

"Hold it," said Seth. "We never decided we were going to make this our adventure. We haven't agreed on anything. Remember, we had said everyone had to agree. This could be too risky. If Mom and Dad ever found out about this…"

"Is that a threat? You gonna run to Mom and Dad." Pete grabbed his pillow and swung it at his brother, hitting him on the arm.

Ouch. Even I felt that, although Seth didn't yell out.

"I never said that." Seth picked up his own pillow, and the pillow fight was on.

"Stop it, stop it!" I yelled, and stepped out of harm's way just before one of the pillows ripped apart, scattering feathers around the room. Some even floated out the window.

"You would love a pillow," his brother snapped.

"Help me get these feathers picked up before Mom and Dad get back."

"That's your pillow; pick up your own feathers, squealer."

Fuming, Seth picked up a pile of feathers off the bed and threw them at Pete, who ducked.

The feathers landed outside with a loud clunk.

Pete grabbed a handful of feathers from the floor and threw them back at his brother, and the fight resumed. I went to the window and looked out.

Feathers should not go *clunk.*

Chapter 4

At the window I got a good view of the porch roof below. No wonder the feathers had gone clunk—Seth had scooped up his e-reader along with the feathers and thrown the whole pile out the window. This was going to be very, very bad.

"Hey, Seth," I said, "you'd better get over here." I pointed to the ledge outside the window.

He spotted his reader down below.

"I don't believe it. Now look what you made me do. I lost my first one a week after getting it for my birthday. Now this. If this one is broken, Dad will have my head on a platter."

Pete and I started to laugh. It was kind of mean and I knew it, but we couldn't help ourselves, seeing the look on Seth's face. He didn't know whether to laugh or cry. He stood there running his hand through his hair and biting on his lower lip.

"You both think it's funny. Someone has to get out there and get it. And you know that I can't do heights. I won't go out there. You gotta help me."

"I'm too big to crawl out onto the ledge," said Pete.

I looked over at Pete. He had gotten bigger and taller. And I never realized how cute he was. I caught myself staring, and my cheeks felt warm. I turned away and blurted out, "I'll fit out there." I turned back to see the twins eyeing each other.

"Oh no. No," said Pete. "It's too dangerous. What if you fell off?"

"Stop being such a wimp, it'll be easy. Trust me. I can belly crawl along the roof if you both hold my feet. As soon as I grab the reader, I'll yell 'got it' and you can pull me back in."

"Not happening," blurted out Pete loudly. "I won't let you do it." Seth and I fell silent at Pete's emotional outburst. "What? It's too risky. Look at the slope of the roof. We better wait for our dad to come home. He'll know what to do."

"No way," said Seth. "If Dad finds out, I'll never get another one. I already lost one e-reader. She can do it. Like she said we'll hold on tight to her feet. Right, Kate?"

My brain was working overtime, and I seized the moment. "Only if you agree to the adventure." I folded my arms across my chest and looked him right in the eye, waiting for his answer.

"That's blackmail," said Seth. "You could go to jail for that."

I smiled at Seth, not saying a word, but added a tap to my foot.

"Yep," said Pete, catching on, "you have to agree to go along with us."

Seth cherished his reader, but wasn't known to give in easily. So I played along with him for his answer. But he took too long, so I called his bluff, "Okay, I gotta go," and started to leave.

"Oh, okay, I'm in," said Seth, kicking the chair. "Now let's get my reader."

Seth was so predictable. "We better hurry," I said. "My dad's probably wondering where I am.

I looked out the window at the dirty ledge. Chills coursed through my body as I looked down at the steep roof covered with leaves and feathers dancing around. It had gotten cooler out, and the wind had picked up. I was numb from fright by the time the twins tied rope around my ankles. It was pretty scary out there, although I'd never admit that to the twins. I slipped out the window on my belly. The twins took hold of my feet, and I crawled along the ledge, praying they wouldn't let go. I went slow and glanced down. I saw the trampoline. It had rained last night and the ledge was still wet. As I shimmied along, my clothes helped soak up some of the water and the feathers stuck to me. I looked like a bird in distress. Although it wasn't that cold out, I felt chilled from my wet clothes. It is a good thing I wore pants this morning. As I crawled closer to my target my confidence built up. I can do this.

"Almost there," I called back and reached out for Seth's e-reader. "Got it," I yelled in an excited voice, holding up the reader. The twins hurriedly pulled back on my shoes, and both my feet popped out of them. I slid faster and faster toward the edge of the ledge.

The twins screamed along with me as I went flying off.

I landed on the trampoline down below, with the reader triumphantly in hand against my fast-beating heart. Gosh, was I glad I took gymnastics. No one had told me how useful a backward flip would come in handy someday.

Relief was plastered all over the twins' faces when they saw me safe as I jumped around and laughed. "I'm glad this was here," I said, out of breath. At the same time I remembered when I thought of quitting gymnastics. After today, I was sure glad I didn't.

Seth got on the trampoline. "Give that back to me before you break it," and he grabbed his reader from my hand. He didn't waste any time checking that it still worked, then jumped around a few more times before hopping off.

Seth could be pretty selfish. Not even a "thank goodness you're okay and thanks for saving my e-reader." Nope, it was all about him. True, he'd be in trouble if it had broken, but still...

"You okay?" asked Pete. "Gosh, that was scary when you slid off the roof. I didn't know what to think. Then I remembered the trampoline out here. I had my fingers crossed you'd land on it. No more roof tricks please. You could have been killed."

"But she wasn't," said Seth, "and my reader is working fine. Good going, Kate."

"Hey," I said, in between jumps, "I've missed this thing. It's fun. Wish I had one around last summer."

"Geez, doesn't anything scare you?" asked Seth. He practically threw my shoes back at me when I got off the trampoline.

My stomach answered for me. It let out a loud growl.

It was embarrassing, but it got Seth to laugh. Then we all laughed. "I gotta go. See you guys tomorrow."

Returning to a quiet cabin was unsettling. Dad was alone in his office upstairs, pecking away at his computer. Not a good time to interrupt him. Something I learned a long time ago when I was a toddler. He loved the solitude here in the mountains. He said it was a great place to write. If he hadn't kept the cabin, I never would have seen the twins again and have our summer adventures. My mom didn't miss it here. Europe had become her favorite summer getaway since the divorce. As for the rest of the year, she would have sold our house in Connecticut and moved to a place in Manhattan if it wasn't for me. At least my feelings were considered *somewhere* in their separation. Although, if you forced me to admit it, I might confess the old house was lonely without my dad.

My mom was always tucked away in her home office. There was hardly ever any mommy-daughter time. My dad and I had kidded around a lot. I didn't do that with my mom. She was not a kidder. She was a late worker. Real late. We had dinner together every night, though. Daughter time. Now there was *Mike*.

Mike ate at our house a lot.

Mike took Mom out for dinner a lot.

Mike made it so I was stuck with my old nanny a lot.

I was not a Mike fan.

Tonight's dinner had me sitting at the table with my dad and Lily, listening to their conversation while admiring

Lily's red nails. That was the only thing I liked about her. She'd cooked up some Swedish dish. Actually it wasn't too bad, but no compliments came from me. My dad had said enough for the two of us.

The following morning, I found Pete and Seth on their deck. Seth with his nose in his e-reader, and Pete throwing pebbles into the lake. They certainly weren't ready to process girly stuff like nails. But this mattered.

"What do you think of fancy nails? Good or bad?" I asked.

"Uh, I…" said Seth.

"They…well…" uttered Pete.

"I mean, why do guys think girls who are all dolled up are so special?" I became instantly self-conscious of my ratty cut-offs and holey sneakers, but I'd opened this can of worms and I wanted to see it through. I caught Seth sneaking a look at Pete and rolling his head sideways. Then Pete looked at me.

"We don't think about nails. C'mon, let's go." He sounded eager to get started.

It didn't look like the nails were of any interest to them. Maybe if I polished my nails red they'd have something to say.

"Seth, move it," said Pete. "We're leaving."

"Almost," said Seth, "let me just finish this chapter. Only got a couple more pages."

Pete stormed over to Seth. "Cut it out. Finish it later." Seth really knew how to push Pete's buttons, and the last thing I wanted was them bickering.

"Yeah, let's move it," I said, joining in. We hovered over him with our hands on our hips. Seth got that we were mad. His hands went up in surrender.

"Okay, okay, hold your horses." He slammed his book down. "Okay, ready to migrate." He flashed a big grin at us.

"I brought a small notebook along to keep track of things," said Pete. He wrote down the date, and day, and said he planned to put the rest in when we got there.

Pete's notebook impressed me. First, that he was as curious as I was, and second his wanting to keep the notes told me he was serious about this adventure. I wished it would rub off on Seth.

I led with Seth behind me and Pete bringing up the rear. Along the way the sweet-scented native azaleas masked the hot and muggy day that it was. I stopped when I spotted the tree house.

"Let's hide our bikes here," I said. "These bushes are close to the path leading to the tree house. If Joe's not there, we could start our snooping. Whatta you think, guys?"

"Fine," said Seth wiping his forehead. "Whatevs."

"Good idea," said Pete with enthusiasm, already taking notes about something. He didn't seemed bothered by the heat and humidity. It was probably eighty to ninety degrees out.

"Okay, let's synchronize our watches," I said. "Mickey says it's 4:40 p.m."

"You still wearing that Mickey Mouse watch?" asked Seth. "You're a teenager now."

"I think it's kinda cute," said Pete. "Nothing wrong with wearing Mickey on your wrist. We still have our old ones. Maybe I'll wear mine next time too," he said, smiling at me.

"Oh, so now we're in the Mickey Mouse club. C'mon, get real." Seth nodded his head sideways, rolling his eyes. I was surprised by how annoyed that was making me. I could almost hear Mom going, "Don't you roll your eyes at me, young lady."

"I bet if I wore that, you wouldn't think it was so cute," Seth said.

"What, the Mickey watch?" Why was he going on about that? "Never mind the watch. You're forgetting why we're here. While you two here were clucking like hens, I checked out the tree house. Joe's not up there."

"Let's see, time 4:45. Joe not in tree house," Pete said, and jotted it down next to the date and day.

"Okay, let's go," I said, careful not to make any noise. "Watch where you're walking. I'll lead the way. Try to follow in my footsteps."

As I reached the end of the wall, I peeked around the corner and through the open gate. Bushes lined the ivy-covered walls of a yard the size of a swimming pool. The tree house stood next to the concrete wall. Across the way stood a small cabin with stairs leading up to the door. Grass lined the ground around a circular driveway that I didn't notice before.

"All clear," I whispered behind me and started around the back. "So far, so good—didn't see any activity inside. Okay, guys, you look too."

"Nope," said Pete, scanning the area. "Nothing, maybe they were here earlier."

"Don't see anything," answered Seth, taking a quick peek. "Okay, let's go. They can still be inside the cabin, and we said we're not going inside till we're sure they're not there."

"Wouldn't there be a car inside the gate if someone was here?" asked Pete.

"Not really," I answered. "Nick and Joe were inside that time before waiting for Max. He drove up in a van. Remember? I told you that."

"So how'll we know if they're there or what?" asked Seth.

"It's tough to know unless we see them here and know when they leave," I said. "We have to keep checking. We'll get a good idea after a while when they'll be here. Tomorrow's out. It's July Fourth and my birthday. But after the holiday we can come back. Earlier next time too. Come to think of it, I was here earlier when I saw them all here. Besides, since tomorrow's a holiday, I doubt anyone would be coming back here today or tomorrow. Okay, let's get our bikes." I headed away with my mind already on my birthday. This was my favorite holiday, and being born on July 4th was fun. Everyone celebrated my birthday.

"Can't wait to taste that birthday cake," said Pete, smiling at me. "You get it from that great bakery in Lake Lure. What's its name again?"

"You mean Crumbs. Yeah, I'm pretty sure Dad ordered it from them," I said. "At least I hope so. Before, Mom had done the ordering."

"I can taste that cake now," said Seth. "The thought of it makes my mouth water. Yummy."

"D-I-E-T," taunted Pete.

I was about to get all in a huff that he would dare tell me I needed to diet when Seth spouted off.

"Shut up about my weight. It's none of your business. I'll eat all the cake I want."

"Yeah, I bet you will. Oink, oink."

"But nobody diets on July Fourth," I said. "It's my birthday. You have to share my cake with me." That quieted them down.

When we reached the twins' cabin, we fist-punched goodbye.

As much as I wanted to return to the tree house, I couldn't wait for tomorrow. I'm not sure why I was so excited about my birthday present from my dad. He'd already hinted at what he was giving me. Dad was so into books that that's the only thing he could think of giving. Another collector's something or other. I still hoped he might have gotten the hints I'd been dropping. But when I saw a package the shape of a book with a ribbon around it in his office, I assumed that was my present.

Not what I wanted.

Chapter 5

I wish I could do this every morning. Just jump up and get out of bed. I already knew that answer. But every day wasn't my birthday and a holiday. It was motivating to wake up to presents.

Waffles for breakfast, the Fourth of July, and—my birthday! A yummy day. The best day of summer. As I strolled into the kitchen for my dad's annual Belgian waffles feast, I promised myself I would try to forget Lily was there instead of my mom. With the tree house and cabin taking up the rest of my thoughts, I figured that'd be easy enough. I had always looked forward to this day and the party at night at a neighbor's cabin. Afterward we'd watch the fireworks light up the sky. When I was little, I thought the fireworks were special for my birthday.

Lily and my dad were already in the kitchen. They were discussing something about his book.

My birthday gift was on the breakfast table. It wasn't the box I'd seen in his office or a flat box like the kind my mother always gave me with a shirt or jeans inside. This box was small and rectangular. It's the right size. I'm old enough. It's gotta be it. Oh, *please, please,* let it be it.

Waving his spatula in the air, my dad winked at me. "Go for it, Kate."

I tore at the paper, opened the box, and held my breath. Through tears, I looked at my first smartphone.

"Yes!" A zillion hints was just the right amount. My fist punched in the air and my dad came over with the spatula in his right hand and high-fived me with the other.

"Oh! Dad, thank you, thank you," I cried, hugging him.

I couldn't wait to tell my mom and take pictures with the camera in the phone.

Lily took an envelope from her pocket and handed it to me. She bent down and gave me a hug and wished me a happy birthday. That was a first.

Before even opening it, I kinda knew what was inside. Lily being an editor would probably give a gift certificate to Amazon. I had guessed right and that was fine with me.

Shortly after breakfast, I joined my dad and Lily for my family's annual 4th of July trail ride with friends. They owned a stable in Lake Lure, about twenty-five minutes away from our cabin.

Hank, the owner, was super nice. I'd known him forever. He let me pick the same horse every year. Racer was gorgeous and a total sweetie. We were pals from the beginning. As soon as I stepped outside it felt like I was walking through a sauna. My shirt was already stuck to my back. The mountains were usually cooler, but July was the hottest month and today was hot and sticky. I made a mental note to not forget extra bug spray tonight.

Trail riding was something I had always looked forward to when I was younger. But since I'd started riding English style, I was not amused by the Western saddle, which meant riding at a slower gait. Perfect for a recreational trail that's a nature ride and doesn't involve speed, form, or skill. With my dad on my one side and Lily on the other, I clomped along between them as if I was a prisoner and they were my guards. My hands were still sore from earlier and it hurt to hold my reins.

Lily had trouble getting on the horse, and the way she held the reins told me that she knew nothing about riding. Yep! Lily was definitely a city girl. I bet she couldn't wait to get back to her books and New York. Made me wonder what Lily did all those times she told about when she'd come up to the mountains visiting relatives. She sure must have read a lot because she certainly never learned to ride a horse.

I guess the thought of a canter was out of the question. Being a good rider, I tried to keep my sighs of boredom to myself.

Lily and my dad went on blabbering about books and stories and left me out again. My mind wandered to what I really wanted to think about anyway: the tree house and the cabin. I thought of the men, and the question arose: What were they doing with all those boxes? What were they doing with guns? Something was definitely up. I just had to find out what.

I returned from trail riding and made a beeline for my new phone. The red charging light had turned green. Now all I needed to do was program it.

That evening I brought my cell phone with me to my neighbor's July 4th party.

Flickering candles illuminated the center of the round tables. A large group of my neighbors were gathered on the lawn. I posed for some pictures before taking my first pictures with my new phone.

I inhaled the aroma of the hot dogs and hamburgers on the grill. I saw corn on-the-cob still in their husks. Something else I missed out on last year. Couldn't wait to dig my teeth into one. A cloth of red, white, and blue gave the buffet table a patriotic look. July 4th was always pot-luck. Space was left in the center of the table for my birthday cake.

As I walked around the buffet table, I saw the twins stuffing their faces with chips.

"Caught you," I said, coming up behind Pete. He startled, yanking his hand back and flinging the chips all over Seth.

"Hey, watch it," yelled Seth, who picked up the chips and threw them back at Pete.

I recognized the beginning of a chip fight and went into action. "C'mon, guys. Didn't mean to scare you, Pete. I'm sorry. I'm surprised you guys got here so early."

"Yeah, well, Pete couldn't wait to get here. He got ready earlier tonight. Never did that before, but I know why."

"You do not and so what," said Pete. "What's wrong with looking nice. You didn't even change your shirt. It's not nice coming to Kate's party looking like that."

"It wasn't dirty, bro. Why should I change it? I look fine. I'm not trying to impress anyone."

Ignoring his brother, Pete turned to me and continued. "You look pretty. Hey, I never saw you with earrings on before."

Seth edging back into the conversation said, "I love being here on July Fourth. Last summer the fireworks were so cool. We went to the same spot farther down the lake where you could really get a good view. Sorry you missed it. Did you celebrate in Switzerland?"

"Nope, it's not their holiday. I missed being here with you and seeing the fireworks."

Pete started to say something, but was interrupted...

"Coming through, watch it, kids. I know you wouldn't want me to drop this."

Everyone close by parted the way as two men held a huge cake and placed it in the center of the table.

The twins' eyes widened when they saw the cake that was decorated with red, white, and blue icing, and big red roses all around it and on top. Written in script on the cake was *Happy July 4th* and below that in script was *Happy Birthday Kate*. Below that stood two large candles in the shape of the number thirteen.

Pete smiled at me. "Happy birthday, Kate. Now you're a teenager too."

"What did your dad give you for your birthday?" asked Seth.

"A smartphone!" I whipped it out of my pocket and held it up to the twins. "Stand close together, and I'll get a picture of you."

Pete grabbed Seth's shoulder and touched their heads together. He crossed his eyes and held up two fingers behind Seth's head.

"So how many presidents were born on July Fourth?" Pete taunted, like I wouldn't know the answer.

"Calvin Coolidge," I said, thinking, Everyone knows that. Then again, maybe not.

Pete was surprised that I knew the answer. He folded his arms and gave me a cocky look.

"Bet you don't know where he was born and what year?"

Before I had a chance to answer, Seth blurted out, "Plymouth, Vermont, in 1872."

Pete punched his brother in the arm. "Hey, bookworm, I wasn't askin' you."

"Yeah, you're asking your girlfriend," he mumbled loud enough to be heard.

"Back off, jerk," said Pete, and threw a fake punch at his brother.

A bell rang signaling time to eat.

The twins piled their plates high with food. It amazed me that they could carry them. That led me to thinking. The way the evening was going, a food fight was probably coming, and they had plate loads of ammo.

After everyone had eaten and it was getting dark, I went with the twins to catch fireflies. As a small child my dad carried me on his back as I tried to catch the fireflies with my small net.

"When are you going to get rid of that net?" asked Seth. "You're a teenager now."

"It's easier to catch them with. Besides, I get more fireflies this way. You should try using a net," I said. "You might like it."

"They're fireflies, not butterflies," said Seth. "Try it without the net."

"We like catching them with our hands," said Pete, "and pulling out the green light when it's lit."

"Yeah, I know you do. That's gross and mean."

"Got one," Seth called out and joined his brother and me.

Someone called out for me. "Kate, time to cut the cake."

I hurried over to the table, where the number thirteen candle flickered in the soft breeze.

Lily was standing next to my dad at the table. It felt awkward seeing Lily there and not my mom. Everyone sang Happy Birthday to me. I made my wish and blew out the candles.

My mom had always cut the first piece. Now that I was thirteen and my mom wasn't there, I figured I'd do that. I reached out for the knife the same moment Dad picked it up and handed it to Lily. I closed my eyes and pictured my mom standing there. But when I opened them it was still Lily.

Certain that everyone there had read my thoughts and sensed my embarrassment, I no longer wanted any birthday cake. I walked away. How could he? How could my dad have done that to me? My dad called me back, but I kept on going and felt the glare of his eyes on my back.

As I walked along the lake, I felt my first mosquito bite of the evening. I'd forgotten to use bug spray. The thought of lots of mosquito bites was interrupted by the noisy crickets chirping and the cicadas clicking. They were out in full force tonight. Maybe they were celebrating the holiday too.

When I sauntered back to the party, I saw Pete swipe one of the red roses from my birthday cake, gobble it up, and lick his fingers. Seth had cut himself another piece. I caught him wrapping it up and sneaking it inside his jacket pocket. I wondered how many pieces he had already eaten. Hope someone saved a piece for me. As I started toward them, I heard the first loud boom of the evening and looked up. The first sparks of fireworks shot across the sky. "Let's go," I shouted. The three of us raced to grab our favorite spot on the lake to watch the fireworks.

Seth ran ahead and staked out our spot on the grass. Pete plopped down next to him and motioned for me to sit next to him.

"Kate always sits in the middle," said Seth. "Here you go." He patted the ground for me to sit between them.

"She's a teenager now," said Pete, "and can sit where she wants."

I'd already grabbed a spot next to Pete. "I'm good," I said, relieved as a display of our flag burst open in the sky, ending the discussion.

"That cake was sure good," said Pete, whose face still had a speck of icing on it.

With my finger, I swiped some onto his nose and we both giggled. Pete blushed.

"Cut it out, you two," yelled Seth. "I thought we came to watch the fireworks."

Pete and I looked at each other and giggled again only

silently this time.

Throughout the evening, out of the corner of my eye, I caught Pete stealing glances my way. I tried not to notice, but when I turned my head and caught his eye, he sheepishly smiled at me. I smiled back.

That's when the fireworks started on the ground. Seth smashed the piece of cake he had saved into Pete's face.

"What the... Seth, I can't believe you did that," said Pete. "What's wrong with you?"

It was hard not to laugh. Pete looked like a clown with birthday cake all over his face.

"What am I supposed to use for a towel," said Pete. He grabbed Seth's shirt to wipe his face.

"Cut it out!" Seth shouted. "Use your own shirt." He yanked away and they glared at each other. "What?" Seth finally asked. "You love icing and this was from Kate's birthday cake. You wanted my share, right? Well, now you got it."

"What we got is wasted birthday cake," I interrupted. "C'mon, guys, stop messing around and sit down. We're missing the fireworks. Sit here, Seth." I patted the ground next to me. Pete took the other side. Like old times, I sat between them. By the end of the evening both twins acted like nothing happened earlier.

Chapter 6

I slept late the morning after my birthday, and boy did it feel good. I found my dad in the kitchen with Lily. As soon as they saw me they stopped talking.

"Hey, Dad, do you have a minute? My computer's acting funny."

"Not now, Kate. I'm busy here with Lily. Can it wait till later?"

"I'll only take a minute. Why can't Lily wait?"

My dad shot me a look. You know, the kind that said, Knock it off, young lady. I also picked up that my dad would have more to say about this later.

This left me with a bitter taste in my mouth. You could have asked me what the problem was. I couldn't remember feeling this alone.

According to Mickey sitting on my wrist, it was too early to meet up with the twins, so I decided to read for a while. Reading wasn't my favorite hobby of all time, not like it was with Seth, but sometimes nothing hit the spot like a good story.

Pete was good at telling good stories. He was good at a lot of things, come to think of it. Especially making me smile.

It kind of freaked me out where my thoughts were going. I pulled a book from my bookcase and got lost in someone else's life, only coming back to this one when my stomach growled.

That made me think of tonight. Dinner in downtown Asheville and a movie afterward. At least this was the plan before this thing with Dad. I'd eaten out a lot since my parents separated.

I missed the dinners at home we used to have when we were a family. Mostly that happened on weekends with my parents being so busy. There was a time when we laughed a lot at those dinners, sometimes at the silliest things.

This past year, there was tension in the room when my parents were together. Sometimes I caught them arguing when they thought I wasn't around, but eventually it didn't matter if I was there or not. I had school friends whose parents were divorced. But I never thought I'd be in that club until the night my parents broke the news.

That night had been rotten. I had to sit there, sandwiched in between them, while they told me.

Numb was the only way to describe how I felt. I don't know why I was so shocked to hear that they were splitting. Part of me knew that it was just a matter of time. They bickered constantly.

"Kate," my mom had said that night, patting my hand. "Your father and I have made a decision to live apart. We both love you very much. This is something between us and not anything you did."

I had slumped into my dad's arms and couldn't stop crying. He'd kissed my forehead and whispered into my ear how much he loved me, and that nothing would ever change that. He went on to say that he would be moving into our summer house. That we'd see each other on holidays, and I'd spend my summer vacation there like I always did. And, of course, I could always call him to talk. "Anytime," he had said. What he should have said was "except when Lily's around."

My dad had walked me to my room and sat with me for a while. I must have fallen asleep on the bed. The next morning, I awoke with a blanket over me, and I was still dressed. My dad was gone.

So here I was. Summers here and winters there and shared on Christmas and Thanksgiving. New luggage had been one of my Christmas gifts last year. It wasn't even on my Christmas list. Duh! How stupid I'd been. The hints were all around.

And now here I was, stuck with Lily when it was supposed to be The Summer of Kate and Dad. I couldn't stand her.

I was gathering my rock collection together when my dad asked for a few minutes of my time. His way of saying, I want to talk to you, young lady! Here it comes!

"Lily is a guest of mine," he said. "I expect you to be respectful to her. I didn't like your tone of voice. In fact, I don't like your behavior since she's been here."

"Well, Dad, this was supposed to be *my* vacation time

with you, and you only want to spend time with Lily. Lily this, Lily that."

"Stop that right now. Look, I know this separation hasn't been easy on you, but when you're older you'll understand. You need to accept the fact that your mom and I are not getting back together. Your mom has a new friend. Well, Lily is my new friend."

"I thought so," I said. "I knew it. She's not here with you to work on your book. She's your new girlfriend. I saw the way you look at her. Well, she's *not* my mother."

"Of course she's not. She's not trying to be. But can't you be friends with her? She had nothing to do with what went wrong in our marriage. Why don't you give her a chance?"

A river of tears welled up inside me. Like a broken dam, they poured out of me. By now I was on my knees rocking back and forth. My face was in my hands. My dad had knelt down beside me. I pushed him away.

"Please!" he said. "Look, I never meant to hurt you. I know that things aren't exactly the same as before, but it's going to take some time getting used to everything. I'll always be here for you. I love you, sweetheart." Then he kissed the top of my head and gave my shoulder a squeeze.

"Don't forget," he said. "Your grandparents are coming soon to visit. They've been looking forward to seeing you." He got up to leave then stopped at the door. "I want you to know that I have been looking forward to spending time with you while your mother is in Europe."

I kept my back to my dad and waited for him to leave. "Careful biking, Kate," he said, and left the room.

I stood up from the floor and grabbed my rocks and left the house, slamming the door behind me. Dad hated when I did that.

The twins were riding in circles outside their cabin. I slipped on my sunglasses to cover my red-rimmed eyes. I didn't want to have to explain why I'd been crying. Not right now anyway.

"Brought something to show you," I said, and opened the box holding up my rock collection.

"Did they fall out of your head?" asked Seth, who thought that was funny and couldn't stop laughing.

"Knock it off," said Pete. "Let's see 'em."

I offered him a rock.

"That jagged pitch-black one is cool," said Pete. "I like fractured rocks." I lifted it out and handed it to him.

Seth slapped his arm around his brother. "That's because you're fractured."

"Hardee-har-har." Pete turned and threw an imaginary rock at Seth. "Gotcha," he said when he ducked.

Then Seth pointed to a waxy-looking rock in the box. "I'll take that one." He reached over and grabbed it before I could hand it to him.

"That's a neat one. It's called a soft rock."

Seth squeezed it. He squeezed it again. "You're crazy, this is hard."

"I know, but that's what it's called. Okay," I said. "Ready to go? I can't wait to check out that place."

"Go where?" asked Seth, acting like he didn't know

what I was talking about.

"Ignore him," said Pete. "He thinks he's funny."

"Yeah," said Seth, "I'm ready. Let's migrate. Gosh, you guys can't take a joke."

I put the other rocks back inside my pack, and we biked to the cabin. The twins stayed back as I went ahead and checked if Joe was in the tree house. He wasn't.

I signaled the twins and they came forward. We left our bikes in our usual hiding place and approached the tree house. No noise could be heard. No car inside the gate. I dashed over to the small gate. Again, it swung open at my touch. Yes! "C'mon, guys," I whispered.

"Hey, we're not going in there," said Seth. "We're supposed to be scouting the place out. How do you know someone's not in there?"

"Seth's right," said Pete. "We need to check things out more before going inside the compound. Even if they're not there, maybe they're on their way."

"But, guys, we're already here. A quick look. Then we're gone. C'mon, we're wasting time."

At the same moment a noise startled me. "Is that a car?" I said. "Hurry, guys, we'll hide inside." I ran in, expecting the twins to follow, but they didn't.

Through the bars of the big gate, I saw them run to the other side of the road. Oh, no. Were they crazy? There was poison ivy in there. I hoped they knew what that looked like. I was tempted to yell out to them, but the gate's squeaking stopped me. What was I thinking? I scurried behind some large bushes where I wouldn't be seen.

The gate squeaked open and the black van drove

through. It stopped in front of the cabin about twenty-five feet away from me. That gave me a good view of both from my hiding place.

I quickly took out my cell phone and brought up my camera. Fighting off mosquitoes, I waited for the right moment, and took my first picture.

A man got out of the van. I recognized Nick. Then Joe climbed out after him. *Click.* I became aware of another man whose gruff voice and abrupt manner were hard to mistake. With all those tattoos it had to be Max. He shouted orders at Nick and Joe. *Click.*

Joe headed toward the tree house. Nick opened the back of the van and unloaded some boxes. *Click.* Max walked over to the cabin. He pulled a chain from his pocket. A bunch of keys dangled from it. He rattled them around until he found the one he wanted. Then he opened the cabin door and went inside. *Click.*

Nick unloaded more boxes and carried them inside the cabin. Several minutes passed before he came back out. He reached for another box, but it wouldn't budge. He had his arms wrapped around it and yanked on it. It suddenly loosened and he danced backward, toppling to the ground.

The bottom of the box had split open. Packages wrapped in white paper, the size of paperback books, tumbled out. They scattered around the ground. *Click. Click. Click.*

Nick rushed around gathering up the packages.

The last package was scooped up and re-loaded inside the larger box. He removed some tape from inside the van and closed the big box back up. Then he leaned back against the van with one knee bent. He raised his arm and wiped his face with his shirt. Then he pulled a cigarette from his pocket, lit up, and inhaled a long puff. It looked like he swallowed the smoke, and I caught a whiff of something that had a smelly odor, like a skunk. I thought I recognized the smell from another time, and realized he was smoking pot.

Before standing up, Nick's head rested against the car, and his eyes closed for a few moments. Then he crushed the weed out with his foot and looked around. Lifting up the pile of boxes in his huge arms, he used his elbow to slam the door shut and wobbled inside.

I kept still and waited. But I knew I couldn't wait too long. The sky was darkening and thunder boomed. I could smell the rain and knew any moment it was going to come. According to my phone, fifteen minutes had passed when the cabin door finally opened. I got a shot of Max as he stepped out of the cabin, got into the van, and headed toward the gate.

A couple of minutes later Nick left the cabin. He walked in the direction of the gate, followed by Joe.

"Get to work on that gate," Nick ordered. "You're lucky that Max never saw it unlocked."

A few minutes later, Joe appeared with some tools and a paper bag.

He emptied the bag on the ground, and I heard something jingle. Probably the new lock and keys. Just as Joe reached out for the gate's knob, Nick called out.

"Joe, I need your help here. Hurry!"

Joe dropped everything on the ground and rushed back

to the cabin.

A few minutes passed. I sat still, afraid even to blink, but no one came back out. I couldn't stand it. What were they doing inside?

I skulked over to the cabin window. I kept low below the ledge and listened for any noise from inside. When I didn't hear anything, I crossed my fingers and glanced within. I knew I was taking a big chance and Joe could come out anytime.

A few boxes sat inside on the cabin floor. Then I blinked. The door on the other side of the room from the window swung open facing me. I ducked down so fast that my head hit the ledge.

Someone was coming out!

Chapter 7

No one could have heard me when I yelled "Ow." I couldn't even hear myself. Because at the same time, flashes of lightning erupted in the sky followed by cracking thunder. Still, I crouched under the window ledge with one hand over my mouth and the other holding the top of my forehead where I smashed it. It throbbed. I kept my arms up, using them as my umbrella as I huddled against the cabin wall and waited.

When the rain let up, I raised my head. The men were no longer there. My eye caught a red spot under the ledge. *Blood.* I looked at my gooey-red fingers. *My blood.* Getting up was a challenge. I stood up and fell. Again. Then again. Finally, I just crawled away from the window to the small gate leading to the road. There, I managed to get to my feet and stay there.

Boy, was I lucky not to get caught by those guys.

My bike stood alone. The twins were gone. No surprise there. Pete didn't like thunderstorms. I bet they had beat it home at the first drop of rain.

By now my curiosity was at a high. What was inside all those packages? What was their destination? Lots of questions and no answers. What's going on?

I needed the twins' help. Not that I couldn't do it alone, I thought. But with my head all messed up, it would be better to have the twins there.

Somehow I got on my bike and pedaled. I hadn't expected the twins would have waited for me outside their cabin, but they did. Maybe they felt guilty deserting me.

Seth looked startled. "Your face is bloody!"

"No, just my head..."

"Just?"

"Well, yeah."

"That's it," said Seth. "I told you. This is too dangerous. We're not going back there. None of us."

"Let me finish! Jeez. As I was saying. I just hit my head on the outside ledge looking into the window. My face is fine." Seth didn't look convinced. "No one hurt me," I said. "I have a little bump, that's all. It was worth it, though: I saw some boxes." I didn't dare tell them that I'd nearly been caught. They'd never go back there with me. "We'll go back, but we'll just keep track of their comings and goings for now. We won't go inside. We can at least do that." Neither one of them said anything. Pete was my best bet. "Pete, come on, you're with me on this, right? You won't leave me hanging."

"How about it?" asked Pete, nodding his head at Seth. "Like Kate said, we'll be real careful."

Seth didn't answer.

"Don't forget you promised to do this," I said. "I got

your e-reader back for you."

"Yeah, I know, but that was blackmail. This isn't a fun adventure. It's a dangerous mission. If we do this and get caught..."

"No one's gonna get caught. We'll be together and look out for each other. When we're sure it's safe, we can make our move. All we need is a little evidence. Then we'll contact the sheriff."

Seth shook his head.

"You promised..."

He gritted his teeth and made a noise that I wasn't quite sure how to interpret. Then, finally, his shoulders fell. "Fine. I have to be crazy to agree to this, but I promised and I'm no liar. I'll do it."

"That's my man," said Pete, patting his back. "What's the next move, Kate?"

"I'll text you later," I said. "Gotta go."

Even though it had stopped raining, I arrived home soaking wet.

"Kate," asked my dad, "what happened to you?"

"I didn't make it back in time. I got caught in the rain."

"That's not what I meant," he said, coming toward me. "Is that blood on your head?"

"Oh!" I said. "I fell off my bike into some bushes. It's nothing."

"I'll decide if it's nothing," he said. "Let me take a look."

"Ow!" It hurt when my dad touched my head.

"Let me give Doc Benson a call. I want him to check that you're okay."

Doc Benson was a retired doctor who lived nearby.

Everyone liked him, not only because he carried lollipops in his pocket for us kids, but he was so nice and cheerful. It was hard not to like him.

Doc rushed over and had me point my finger to my nose, to the left, to the right. All sorts of weird movements before he said I'd be fine. It was only a superficial wound. Then he whipped out a lollipop for me.

But it was what he said next. "Kate, I'd go easy bike riding for a few days. You'll get better a lot faster."

My dad jumped on his remark. "Okay, no biking, young lady, until your head heals."

"Dad," I cried out in protest. "I'll be careful."

"Don't Oh Dad me," he said. "You heard Doctor Benson."

When I went to bed that night it was hard getting to sleep. My head hurt.

Early the next morning, I kicked off my covers and looked outside. Clouds filled the sky and the ground still looked soggy. No biking this morning. Besides, my head was still sore. Although I'd never admit it, I'm sure that would have added on extra days away from biking. I texted the twins that my biking license had been suspended until my head healed. I probably made Seth's day. Not with my head being hurt, but with the fact that he didn't have to go near the cabin and tree house for a while.

They texted me back that they had stepped in poison ivy. No big surprise there. Their mom had washed their clothes and they had washed off with something she got from the pharmacy. So far no sign of a rash or itching.

We had agreed to keep in touch. Maybe by the end of the week we could return to the cabin.

At breakfast, my dad asked Lily about the trunk she bought. "Oh, it's just an old trunk, but I kinda liked it. I bet it's from the early 1900s," Lily said. "It looks like it crossed the Atlantic on a few occasions. They're restoring it now. Then they'll ship it to my condo."

Lily lived on Fifth Avenue. My mom had told me that. Did Dad tell her?

"Maybe I'll become an editor," I said. "Sounds like editors earn good money."

"Kate," interrupted my father. "That's enough!"

"That's okay," said Lily, "but I wish that were true. The condo was an inheritance from my father."

When Lily was talking about the restoration shop, my ears had perked up. "I got a great idea," I suggested. "Why don't we have lunch downtown? Then we can pop in at the shop and Lily can show you her trunk."

I wished I could have taken a picture of the expression on my dad's face as he sat there speechless looking at me.

"Well, I can't go biking," I added, "so I thought it might be fun."

"Sure, great, that sounds good to me." Turning to Lily, Dad asked, "What do you think, Lily?"

Lily threw both hands up in the air. "Let's do it," she said. "I'd love for you to see it. Give me an hour. I need to make a few calls."

"Cool!" I said and went upstairs to read. I'd already gotten through two of the books on my summer reading list.

About an hour later, my dad and I waited outside for Lily. We were headed into town once Lily finished whatever she was working on upstairs.

I remembered my smartphone and ran back inside to get it. On the way back downstairs, I saw that Lily was on the phone again. Grown-ups are always complaining that they have to work during vacation. She was talking to someone on the phone about a book shipment, or paper shipment, or some shipment-y thing. She seemed annoyed—her voice was loud and sounded mean. I'd never heard Lily use that tone before. She was a lot tougher than she appeared. But I suppose you have to be in the publishing business. It's important for books to be shipped on time.

By the time Lily came back down and we reached the shop, there was a sign inside the door that said closed. But I peeked into the window. "I think someone's here," I said. "There's a light on in the back."

I could have sworn Lily gave me an annoyed look. "Well, let's see," she said and knocked on the door. A man came running from the back. When I realized it was Nick, my knees almost gave out from under me. My mind was spinning. The reason I'd suggested coming here in the first place was to see if I could catch Joe here. What was Nick doing here? Wow! What was the connection between the tree house, antique shop, and restoration shop?

Nick opened the door, but didn't pull back the chain to open it all the way. "This shop is only for restoration," he said. "If you have something to be restored, you need to check it in at the Asheville store. We get it from them."

"Yes, I know," said Lily. "Sorry to bother you. You're already restoring a trunk for me. I was hoping I could show it to my friend here. It's the only chance he'll get to see it. I'm having it shipped directly to my home in New York."

Then Nick slid the chain back and allowed us to enter. He gave me a look like he recognized me, but I knew I was just being paranoid. Still it sent my heart racing. Nick pointed to the chairs. "Wait here. What's the name?" he asked and disappeared inside the back room.

"I really should have called first," said Lily. "It doesn't seem like they're used to people knocking on their door."

I decided to sneak a look at the back of the restoration shop. When Nick went back to get the trunk, I got an idea. "I wanted you to see the trunk, Dad. But since I've already seen it, I'm going to check out a shell shop I noticed down the street. I'll meet you back here in five."

As soon as I stepped outside I walked down the street and then circled back. I quickly went through the alleyway next to the shop. Stooping down, I poked my head around the corner. A huge antique truck was unloading antiques in the back. Nothing unusual. I was about to leave when I heard someone say, "Here comes Max."

A black van with dealer plates appeared out of nowhere heading my way. Goose bumps covered my arms.

I ducked back around the wall. The black van pulled up behind the restoration shop.

"Okay, load her up," I heard Max say. "I'll be inside. And hurry, we're running late."

I stooped low on the ground, my heart pumping fast. I snuck another look. Two men loaded boxes into Max's van.

I had to get back to my dad and Lily, but it took a minute before I calmed down and fled from the alley. I arrived in front of the store at the same time they opened the door to leave.

"Come on, let's have a nice lunch. You gals hungry?"

"Starving," said Lily. I nodded my head yes, but food was the last thing on my mind. I couldn't wait to get back and text the twins about Nick and Max.

Chapter 8

I texted, "*FLASH!* Spotted Max with Nick today. Why would they be together? What's going on?" A while passed before they texted back with only a bunch of question marks plus "talk soon." Guys could be so weird.

I was without wheels for a few more days. I spent the time reading, and the twins came by a few times. We watched videos in my room, stuffing ourselves on popcorn and puzzling about what could be going on at the cabin and the restoration shop.

Seth still pushed for contacting the sheriff. It bugged me, and I kept reassuring him everything would be fine.

I celebrated Lily's leaving in two days, but not in front of my dad. My cheers were done in the privacy of my room. What was supposed to have been one week had turned out to be a lot longer. My grandparents were scheduled to arrive shortly. Some summer alone with my dad. Grandpa and Grandma had been coming here for years and had their own friends, so at least I didn't have to hang with them.

Not that my grandparents were awful or anything. In fact, I loved my dad's dad. I always had fun with him. As for my grandmother, she was something else. When I was younger and wrote her letters, she would correct my grammar and send the letters back to me. My mom would roll her eyes and my dad just shook his head. But the nice presents she gave me made up for it. I guessed she loved me despite my grammar mistakes.

After breakfast that morning, I donned my life jacket and took two more jackets along in the canoe with me. We had two canoes. When I was little I had named them Ruby and Canary. I sat in the back of Canary and steered slowly along the lake, heading toward the twins' cabin. They waited by their dock.

"You brought Bird?" said Seth as I stepped out of the canoe. "I love Bird."

"If you mean Canary, then yes," I said, unable to ignore the nickname Seth had given my canoe. "My dad and Lily took Ruby today. We could run into them later."

"I think it's weird that you named your canoes," said Seth.

"You have a name, don't you?"

"Yeah, but I'm glad you weren't around to name me."

"His name is really Bookworm," teased Pete. "I think Canary is kinda cute."

"Oops! Almost forgot to give you your life jackets," I said, and headed back to the canoe for them. Still within earshot of Pete and Seth, I caught their conversation.

"Everything she says is cute to you," said Seth. "Don't tell me you don't have a crush on her."

"Back off, okay. And what if I do? She is kinda cute. You're just jealous. You like her too."

"Get out. I don't have time for girls."

"Right, you're in love with your books. I don't buy that. I've seen you look at her."

I thought about climbing back into Canary and paddling home. Geez, I never realized the twins liked me like that. Well, maybe I suspected Pete did, but no way did I think that of Seth.

"Here you go," I said, interrupting them, and tossed them the life jackets. I acted like I never heard their conversation, and at the same time was thrilled that Pete liked me. I kinda liked him too.

"We won't go too far, just up to the cove and back. You can take turns paddling at the bow. I'll steer from behind."

"Life jackets to go to the cove and back?" asked Seth.

"Yep," I said, "it might be a short ride, but you still need to wear life jackets."

Seth walked toward the canoe. Instead of getting in with his knees bent and holding on to both sides of the canoe, he stepped in. The canoe rocked violently from side to side, about to capsize.

Pete lunged and tried to steady it. Seth stumbled and collapsed on the middle seat and grabbed hold of both sides.

"What's wrong with you Seth?" I yelled. "You know the right way to get into a canoe." He did that on purpose. "That's not funny," I said. "We could have capsized."

Seth squirmed in his seat. "But we didn't," he said, shrugging his shoulders. "Besides, we're wearing life jackets."

This time it was me doing the eye roll.

Pete knelt into the canoe and headed up front when Seth shoved him into the middle seat and grabbed the front seat for himself.

That earned him an arm punch from Pete.

I picked up my paddle. "Ready? Let's go." I steered away from their cabin, and quickly realized I wasn't in cadence with Seth.

Seth knew what to do. He was just being silly. If he thought this was a way to get my attention, he was wrong.

I no sooner thought that when a frog leaped out of the water onto Seth's lap. He cupped his hands to grab the frog, but it escaped into the hull. When Seth jumped up to catch the frog, he lost his balance and tumbled into the water. The canoe pitched from side to side. I felt my stomach plunge. We reached out to help Seth, but that pushed him further into the water.

Seth screamed, "You almost drowned me. Don't touch me, I can do it myself." He kicked his way back into the boat. It nearly capsized the canoe.

"Sit down!" I yelled. "It's not worth getting killed over a frog." The creature leaped around till Pete caught it and put it in a box with a net over it.

"We'll throw it back into the water later," he said.

"Okay," I said, "let's go! Seth, we need to pull at the same time."

"Pull what?" Seth yelled back in an innocent voice.

"You know what pull means," said Pete. "What's wrong with you today?"

Seth turned around and smiled at his brother. "I thought

you liked having fun," he said, enjoying the moment. "At least I thought you'd said that."

I tried to keep the canoe in a straight line. Seth for sure was trying to annoy Pete and me, but I refused to bite. The canoe continued to zigzag, but I handled it okay.

Finally, we docked by a small cove and checked on our little frog, who was croaking like mad. We decided to leave him in the box till we got back home. Then we got out. I was about to yell at Seth, but Pete did it for me.

"Stop being such a brat. I'm sitting in front on the way back. If this is your idea of fun, think again. Kate could get in trouble if something happened to her canoe."

"Nothing happened to it, did it?" asked Seth, still trying to provoke Pete.

"C'mon, let's walk around a bit," I said. "We need to put our heads together. What do you think? First, Joe at the antique shop and now Nick and Max at the restoration shop. Something is going on. Let's start scouting out that restoration shop."

"Here we go," said Seth. "Danger Girl on the loose."

"We're just gonna check the place out when they're not there," I said.

"We're always just going to scout it out," said Seth. "Then you end up wanting to go inside."

"You guys are afraid," I said. They hated being accused of that.

"We're not afraid," said Pete. "Come on, Seth, you said you were cool with this, right? How can we find out what's going on if we don't search."

"I guess," he said, shrugging his shoulders.

Pete put up his hand and fist bumped his brother. "Like I said, you're the man."

On the way back the twins switched seats without a peep from Seth.

We were almost back to their cabin when I saw my dad and Lily riding in Ruby ahead of us.

"That's your dad, isn't it?" asked Pete.

"Yes," I said, and waved to him when we passed by. At the same time without my knowing it, Seth took the frog out of the box and threw it into my dad's canoe, where it jumped on Lily.

Lily shrieked and pushed it off her lap with her paddle.

My dad's look was murderous.

"All of you back away. Where'd that frog come from?" he asked, pointing to us.

Pete and I were speechless. "So sorry, Dad." I whacked Seth on the arm with my paddle.

"Ow," he squelched.

My dad's scowl got darker. "Well, stay far away. Lily, you okay?" he asked.

"Sure, no harm done to me," said Lily in an irritated voice.

"We'll get ahead of you guys," said my dad.

We waved as they took off.

Seth's face was white. "She probably killed it," he whispered. "I saw her hit the poor thing with her paddle. Poor little creature, I hope it didn't get hurt."

I suddenly remembered. When the twins were little, they had a dog. One summer some disturbed kid poisoned the dogs around the area. Both twins were inconsolable, but I especially remember Seth was absolutely heartbroken.

We continued on and out of nowhere, Seth leaned over the side of the canoe, treading water with his hand opposite our paddles. That unbalanced the canoe. I struggled to steer away from the shoreline, but the canoe seemed to have a mind of its own.

"Duck down!" I yelled. We were headed toward a hanging tree branch. I placed my paddle into the water and held it there close to the canoe. Then I reversed sides.

I was happy to see the canoe respond to my movements slowly but surely. My heart was still racing as I raised my head up. The canoe came to a full stop parallel to the shoreline.

The twins sat upright when the canoe stopped.

"What's wrong with you?" Pete punched his brother on the arm. "You can't do that. We almost crashed."

Seth punched his brother back. "I just wanted to see what would happen if I did."

"Well, now you know." I tried to keep my cool as I picked off some twigs that had caught in my hair. Suddenly I felt speechless and sleepy.

What a relief I felt when I dropped the twins back at their cabin with plans to see them the next day. I waved, heading for my cabin.

I was happy to deliver Canary back safely. If I'd damaged Canary, I bet my dad would have grounded me from canoeing forever.

What a day!

Chapter 9

The following morning, I met up with the twins at their cabin. Today was recon day. Just thinking about it last night made it hard to fall asleep. We were going to start buckling down and do some real investigating.

They rode their bikes in circles waiting for me. "We've decided something," said Pete as soon as he saw me. "You should contact the sheriff."

I put my hands on my hips. "Oh. You decided, did you?"

Pete seemed to cower a bit. He was letting Seth talk him into stuff.

"Like I told you guys, we need to get our evidence first."

"Yeah, well....you're right." Pete nodded in agreement. Seth rolled his eyes. Of course.

All at once I lost patience. "Follow me." They had a hard time keeping up with me. My new bike was fast, and I was done coddling them. There was evidence to be collected, *then* we'd go to the sheriff. It was that simple.

I stopped a short distance from the trail and stared through my binoculars at the tree house.

Joe wasn't there. I motioned for the twins to get back and signaled for them to wait as I checked out the gate. I didn't see any cars.

"Okay," I said, returning to the twins. "Nothing seems to be going on. Let's go on to the restoration shop."

"Hold up, guys," said Pete. "I need to keep a record when they're here or at the shop." He flipped open his notebook and, talking out loud, wrote down the day, date, and time, and added a note—Joe not in tree house.

A couple of blocks from the restoration shop, a black van appeared in front of us. I recognized the dealer plates. I held up my hand for the twins to slow down, then pointed to the van ahead.

It drove one block past the restoration shop before turning right at the corner.

"What's up," asked Seth. "Why'd we stop?"

"That black van. It belongs to Max. I saw it at the cabin and the restoration shop."

"Where they goin'?" asked Pete.

"Probably around to the back of the shop," I said. "We'll go through the alley. But we shouldn't all three go at the same time. One of us has to stay behind in case."

"In case what?" asked Seth. "You think something's gonna happen, don't you?"

"Nothing's going to happen. Will you calm down? Sheesh. Even on TV you see the police split up. We'll be fine."

"I'll go with her," said Pete. "You wait here. We'll be right back."

"What gives you the right to go first? You wait here."

"Because I'm older. I get to go first."

"What kind of rule is that? You're a minute older."

"Exactly! You can go first next time."

"Make it fast," said Seth, kicking his bike's tire.

We rode through the alley in tandem. I peeked around the wall and whispered back that the van was loading antiques, including some trunks. Then my eye picked up on a trunk that had lots of colorful labels and a dent that looked like an arrow. *Lily's trunk*? But Lily's trunk had already been shipped out. How weird to find another one just like it.

Pete tapped me on the shoulder and interrupted my thoughts. I swung around and got caught totally off guard when he planted a quick kiss on my lips.

"That's for your birthday," he said.

It happened so fast. I blushed, then almost giggled out loud.

Pete had just kissed me.

Pete. My friend for, like, forever. Had kissed me.

Sweet, nice, cute Pete.

Wait a minute, why the heck was he kissing me *now*?

"Oh my gosh, Pete, we're in the middle of a—" I didn't finish because Pete had thrown his hand over my mouth. "Shhh!" he said. Then, whispering, "You've never been kissed before, have you?" Now he blushed.

"Of course I have," I whispered in a stammering voice and stood up. But I hadn't. It was probably pretty obvious.

Pete took a fast peek around the corner and said, "Yep, that's all I see too. Let's go."

We continued through the alley and back to our starting point. But my mind wasn't on the trunks. I couldn't stop thinking of my first kiss. Pete's lips felt so warm and soft.

As we came around the corner, Pete gasped. "Oh no!"

"What?" I said. "What's wrong?"

"Look."

I looked where he was pointing. Seth's bike and e-reader lay on the ground. But there was no sign of Seth himself.

Pete jumped off his bike and ran over and picked up Seth's reader. He clutched it to his chest and paced back and forth. "Seth would never go anywhere without this." His voice trembled. "Something happened to him."

My stomach sank to my knees. Could Seth be one of those kids you read about kidnapped off the street? Pete and I stared at each other. He had a panicked look on his face. I'm sure he saw the same on mine. Was he thinking the same thing?

"The heck with collecting evidence," said Pete. "We need the sheriff."

"Let's not bother him. We can do it ourselves," I said.

"You really think so?"

"I know we can."

Pete said, "I'm going to look around."

As soon as Pete left, Seth strolled around the corner slurping on his drink. I stared at Seth, who acted as if nothing was wrong.

"Hey, what's up? Where's Pete? Whatcha see?"

"You're okay!" I dashed over and threw my arms around him.

"Whatta you mean?" asked Seth. "Of course I'm okay."

By now, Pete, who had been down the street, ran back toward us. In the next moment, he grabbed hold of his brother and pretended to choke him.

"Not funny, Seth. Why'd you do that? You scared the bejeezus out of me. You never go anywhere without your reader."

"Hey, watch it. You made me spill my drink. And what about my reader? It's right here." He patted his back pocket. "Huh!" he said, not feeling anything. "Wow, I had no idea I'd dropped it. Geez, I'm sorry, guys. It's freaking hot. I went around the corner for a soda. Lucky for me you found it. Hand it over."

Pete, about to hand it over, pulled back at the last moment.

"Hey, give it up," said Seth. "It's no good to you. You..."

"What," Pete said, "don't read? I do so. I'd just rather have fun outdoors than be stuck away in some old library."

I piped in, "You really scared us, Seth. I almost called the sheriff."

"C'mon, get over it. So what'd you see?"

"Nothing," said Pete, slapping the reader into Seth's palm.

"We did see something," I said. "We saw a couple of guys unloading big trunks. *Something* is going on with these guys; otherwise, they wouldn't be posting a lookout in a tree. No, those aren't just regular antiques in those crates."

"Bet there's bodies," Seth blurted. "All cut up too, I bet."

"Only you would think of that," I said. "You're sick."

"I'm serious. They're murderers and they hide the bodies in the trunks."

"You read too many mysteries," said Pete. "You'd smell

it if there were bodies. And if they were bodies it would make more sense to put them inside coolers."

"Well, at least I read," Seth said.

Pete shook his head. "I think they're jewel thieves," he said. "Antiques dealers—stolen jewels—the connection makes total sense. Those trunks are full of precious jewels, like the pirates used to do."

"Pirates?" Seth laughed. "Maybe you really should start reading and get acquainted with this century."

The wind picked up. I zipped up my jacket. "We better get going," I said, and headed toward our bikes. Pete and Seth already had their hoodies on. The clouds threatened rain anytime now, and I hoped we'd make it back before the downpour.

"You know what?" I said as we biked home, "I think they could be into smuggling or something like that."

"You mean like a smuggling ring?" Pete added. "Oh, boy. That's serious. What do ya think they're smuggling?"

"Geez, I should have thought of that," Seth said. "I've read about stuff like that. Maybe it's drugs."

"Yeah," I said. "Something like that. We need to check out the cabin and see what we find."

I caught Seth glancing at his brother. Here we go again. "Look, guys, I promise, if we stick together no one will get hurt. As soon as we can collect some solid evidence, we'll go to the sheriff."

"I have a bad feeling about this," said Seth. "They'd have to kill us if they caught us." He turned to his brother. "They'd probably torture us too. I'm not ready to die."

"Yeah, but like Kate said, we'll be real careful."

"We might really be on to something," I said. "We won't go near that cabin if they're there. C'mon, since when don't you like an adventure? What a story to tell your friends back home. You could end up being heroes. And what a book you could write."

"Yeah, we can do something so stupid, we'll end up dead heroes," Seth said.

"Look, guys, don't be afraid. It's no big thing. We'll do a little investigating, and be out of there before you know it."

"Yeah, yeah, give me a sec." Seth scuffed his shoe at the ground. His way of thinking. Finally, he nodded and looked up. "Okay, I'm in, but we better not get caught."

"Great," I said. "We'll check once more and then we should be ready to try to get inside the cabin."

That night after dinner, my dad was alone in the den. I poked my head in. "Got a minute?" I asked. I never did this before, but I closed the door behind me when I entered. No way did I want Lily to hear, although I knew she was upstairs packing, finally. I often wondered if this day would ever come.

"What's on your mind? Why all the secrecy?"

Earlier, I had rehearsed what I was going to say, but now had a hard time getting it out.

"It's Lily," I said, and immediately caught a What about Lily? look on his face. I rushed on. "I was in town today biking with the twins and was surprised to see her trunk in the back of an antique truck. The trunk had lots of labels and a dent in it that looked like an arrow. I was sure it was Lily's." I didn't dare let on about our adventure. But before

I could continue, my dad cut in.

"You thought it was her trunk, but it wasn't. Her trunk was shipped out two days ago. Look, I know you don't like her, but really, isn't this going too far? I mean…" There was a knock on the door.

"Come in?" Dad called. Lily opened the door and stepped inside.

"Oh, sorry," she said. "I didn't mean to interrupt. I'll come back later."

"Stay," said my dad. "Kate was just leaving. We are done, aren't we?"

"Sure," I said, and left his office, ignoring Lily on the way out.

Up in my room, I thought about my conversation with my dad. What hurt most of all was his casting it off as nonsense. Did he really think I was trying to sabotage his precious girl?

During the night, rain tapped against my window. I prayed it would stop before the ground got too soggy, but it was still raining the following morning.

The twins must have been thinking the same thing I was: no biking today. Shoot, I'd come up with some good ideas for our plan, too.

I bet Seth was happy. This meant we had to wait another day to find out what was behind the cabin door. I caught up on more of my summer reading, but my thoughts kept coming back to the tree house and cabin. I prayed for the rain to stop, but it was one more day before it stopped and another to dry up the ground enough for biking. I was tired of reading and watching videos. I wanted to go back to the tree house and cabin and check things out with the twins. It was already the second week of August.

I wondered if we'd ever get inside the cabin.

Chapter 10

After breakfast when I biked to their cabin, Pete seemed pretty upbeat. Seth was in his usual let's get this over with mood and didn't say much.

"Do you think they're at the cabin now?" asked Pete. "It's early, so I'm guessing no."

"Why don't we split up today," I said. "One of us could check out the cabin about the same time two of us snoop around the restoration shop. Let's try to see who is where and when."

"I thought we were all staying together," said Seth. "That was our plan, right?"

"Yeah, but I was thinking, guys. Both of you could check out the restoration shop. If Nick's around he would recognize me from going there with my dad and Lily. You guys wouldn't make him suspicious. I'll handle the cabin. Won't go inside, but I'll wait. I hope that Max shows up. I need to get there before him. Because if he does show, Nick usually runs out to greet him. If Max had any news about a shipment, he would tell Nick before they headed inside the cabin. Gotta get the date of the next shipment."

"Okay, how're we gonna do this?" asked Seth. "What are we looking for?"

"Knock, knock," said Pete, tapping Seth's head. "Anyone home? What do you think we're looking for?"

"You know what I mean," said Seth. "Say the guys are there, is there anything else we should notice?"

"Remember to jot down the time," I said, "what you see in the back of the shop, and who is there. Listen carefully to what they're saying. Go through the alley with your bikes. Make like you're fixing something on your tire in case someone spots you and asks what you're doing there. From what I've seen, they're usually there or at the cabin around this time. Let's meet back at your place in about one hour. This should give us plenty of time to snoop around. If by then they haven't shown, then they're probably not coming today.

"Okay, let's synchronize our watches and get going. Mickey says 11 a.m." I looked at the twins and gave a thumbs-up. "See you later, guys." I turned my bike around.

The closer I got, the faster my heart beat. This was the best summer adventure since coming to these mountains. My dad always said there's safety in numbers. But I didn't mind being alone today. I wasn't going inside the grounds. And the twins should be fine. I liked my idea of fixing their tire if they needed an excuse. As I slowed up and checked the tree house, I saw Joe there.

Darn, they're here already. I've never seen them here

this early. I took out my notebook, jotted down the time, hid my bike behind some tall bushes, and snuck along the side of the wall.

Before I could see anything, I could hear the rumblings of an approaching vehicle. Then the gate opened. I waited till it drove through. Then I took a quick look out and saw the back of a van. Max was here. A car door slammed shut. Boy, it's a good thing I got here now.

"Any news?" asked Nick impatiently. By now I knew his voice too.

"Still not sure of the exact date it's coming in," said Max in a frustrated voice. "Either the end of this week or beginning of next. Will let you know. Then we take care of business, get packed up, and take off. We'll start again in the fall. Too many people around here during the summer. We should have been finished by now. We're lucky we didn't get caught. Can't let this happen again."

I massaged my ear from hugging the wall. Something was going down. Scribbling as fast as I could, I tried to write verbatim what Max had said. *Bingo!*

I ran back to my bike and added more notes in my notebook. Darn, I wish Max had known the date of the shipment. That meant we had to keep close tabs on the cabin for the date and get inside before they were all packed up.

Wait till the twins hear about this! I abandoned the compound and hurried to the restoration shop and found them in the alley. Waving my hand, I signaled for them to come out.

"What are you doing here?" asked Pete. "Time's not up yet."

"Anything going on here?" I asked, doubting it as all the action was at the cabin.

"Nada," said Seth. "So what's up?"

"Well, I have some news. All the men were at the cabin. There's one last shipment and they plan on being all packed up by next week. This info came straight from Max's mouth." Then I read from my notes what Max had said.

"So maybe you're not crazy after all," said Seth. "But now we know there's real danger. We really need to go to the sheriff."

"Seth's right, Kate. It's really getting dangerous."

"Wouldn't that be considered hearsay?" I said. "My mom's an attorney. I've heard her talk about that. Also, I never saw the person talking. Although I'm sure it was Max."

"Hearsay, shmearsay, we should still not go inside that place," said Seth. "That's if we could even get inside. Maybe there's an alarm for break-ins."

"Think," said Pete. "The sheriff and his deputies are the last people they'd want at their cabin."

"Pete's right," I said. "Look, we all agreed to just get some evidence and take it to the sheriff. We're so close. You should start taking notes for your book, Seth."

"If I live to write it," said Seth, shaking his head.

"The only thing that we need to know is the date of the shipment. We're gonna have to stay close to the compound and get inside before that shipment comes. This is it, guys. Let's see what's inside those boxes."

"I can't wait till it's over," said Seth.

"Stop complaining," said Pete. "You got to use your

reader when you weren't on duty."

"Like I really concentrated with you hovering all over the place."

"It's time for lunch and I'm starving," I said. "My dad's cooking outside today on his new barbecue. Why don't you guys come over. There's plenty of food. I know from shopping with him."

"We promised to help our dad with the new shed he's building," said Pete. "Another time, but thanks."

At the twins' cabin, we agreed to meet the next day after breakfast.

That night it was hard falling asleep concentrating on what was in the boxes.

I hurried over to the twins' cabin the following morning. The twins were riding on their bikes.

"Let's go," said Pete, his voice an octave higher than usual.

That's great, I thought. If only Seth would get a little gutsy.

"Okay, guys," I said, "to the cabin. Hopefully, Max's van won't be there. It's when he first arrives that he talks to Nick about everything. That has to happen for us to get the shipment date."

"Do you think he's already there?" asked Pete.

"I think he stops at the cave first. That should give us some time. Where do you think that cave could be?"

The twins shrugged.

"Make sure you have your reader with you, Seth," said

Pete. "I don't want you to get too bored."

"Back off, dork. It wouldn't hurt you to use yours sometime."

"Joe's been the first one I've always seen in the tree house," I said. "That means Nick must be inside. If Max's van isn't around, then we should wait for him to show. Max likes to be out of there way before dark. Let's get moving. We need that date."

When we got there no one seemed to be around. "Let's wait around ten minutes," I said. "If they don't show they're probably not coming today. In the meantime, I want to see if they fixed the gate lock."

We went over to the small gate. Sure enough it had a new lock.

"How are we supposed to get in now?" asked Seth.

Before I could answer, we heard the sound of a car approaching and crouched low along the wall out of sight.

I peeked out and saw the black van stop at the large gate. It passed through and the gate closed.

We waited a few seconds before getting closer to listen. Sure enough, we heard a voice. I recognized Max's thick accent. I couldn't make out exactly what he was saying, but we caught the word "boxes."

I had to get nearer. We crept along the ten-foot-high stone wall surrounding the cabin.

"Boost me up, guys," I whispered. Pete and Seth nodded in agreement. Together, they tried to lift me up, but I fell back on top of them.

They were about to burst out laughing. "Shh!" I slapped my hands over their mouths. "You crazy?" I whispered. "I hope they didn't hear you. Okay, what if you braced your hands together? Let's try that."

I balanced myself on top of them. "A little higher," I called down in a hoarse whisper. "I'm almost there." I stretched my hands toward the top of the wall.

The moment I peeked over the wall, the sound of a gunshot exploded in the air.

The twins' hands jerked upward as I flew over the wall.

Chapter 11

The shrubs on the inside of the wall broke my fall. I found myself buried in ivy and bushes. I lay frozen for a few tense moments, listening, expecting someone to come running over, but it was strangely quiet. The men must have gone inside.

Other than a few scratches on my arms, I seemed to be okay. No broken arm like the last time when I crashed my bike. Where were the bushes then?

I could hear the twins whispering on the other side of the wall.

My attention was grabbed by the sound of twigs and stones crunching beneath a car's tires. It got louder as it moved closer to the gate. An engine idled and the gate opened. An old truck drove through, letting out that gunshot sound. It would have knocked my knees out from under me if I hadn't already been on the ground. It stopped in front of the cabin.

A tall, thin man with long hair stepped out of the truck. I didn't recognize him.

Max came out of the cabin, followed by Nick and Joe. "Hey, Sal, how are the guys doing at the cave?"

"They're finishing loading up the other boxes," said Sal. "They should arrive in about twenty minutes."

What cave? Where? And who are these other guys? My thoughts were interrupted by Max.

"Okay, let's get started," he said. "We shouldn't have to come back here tomorrow." Joe headed to the tree house. Max, Nick, and Sal went inside the cabin.

The door closed and I looked out from behind the bushes. Joe was facing away from me. Time to get out of here pounded inside my head. I braced for my escape.

I commanded myself to get up and run for the gate. Out I went without making any noise.

The kids came running toward me. "Are you okay, Kate?" asked Pete anxiously.

I put my finger to my lips and nodded yes. "Hurry," I whispered. "We need to get back to our bikes and get out of here."

"We're really sorry, Kate," said Pete, "for what happened. When you went over the wall, we wanted to go after you, but a car was coming. We hid. Waited for you. Prayed you'd find a way out. What did happen?"

"Not now," I said. "I'll tell you everything once we get to your cabin. We need to move now." We ran to our bikes and pedaled as fast as we could.

When we reached their cabin, I readied to tell the twins everything. I had pictures of the men. But when I reached for my phone, it wasn't there! I patted down my jacket wildly. It should be there, but it wasn't.

"Oh no, guys, I lost my phone! What if it's at the compound? What if they find it? They'll see the pictures I took and know who we are!"

Seth looked at Kate. "What pictures?"

"You know, the pictures I'd taken of you guys on July Fourth. Those and there were more that I'd taken of the men and the boxes."

"Oh boy!" said Seth. "We're really in trouble if they find your phone. Are you sure you had it on you? Maybe it fell outta your pocket on the bike route. Or maybe you lost it when you fell over the wall."

When you threw me over the wall. The temperature inside me rose. "I have to go back," I said. "I need to find my phone."

"Okay," said Pete. "Let's fly."

"No way," said Seth. "They're probably still there."

"How about just to the trail leading to the tree house," said Pete. "No further. That should be okay."

"Okay, but no further," said Seth. "I'm holding you to it."

"Got it," I said, "let's go."

We walked our bikes so we could search the ground carefully. Pete followed behind me with Seth pulling up the rear. In single file we retraced our steps, each checking what the one in front might have missed.

"Stop," I called back, waving my arm at the twins. I ran over to what I thought could be my phone. But it was only an old wallet. No name. No money.

"False alarm, guys," I called out in a disappointed voice.

We continued down the road. From behind me, I heard

Seth call out. "We're getting too close."

"Sh," I said. "Keep your voices down."

As much as I wanted to go on, I didn't want to do it alone nor chance being seen.

"I was sure I heard them say they weren't going to be here today," I whispered. "We have to come back here tonight."

"You're mad," Seth said. "We'll never find the phone in the dark. Besides, how are we supposed to get inside?"

"You can lift me over the wall again. I can use the ivy to help me climb down. Then I can let you in through the gate."

"That's an adventure on its own," said Pete, flashing his cute smile.

"This is crazy," said Seth. "And like your dad will let you out at night?"

"Who said anything about my dad? I have to sneak out. You too. You're not afraid, are you? We're all in trouble if we don't find the phone. Think about it, guys."

"You said they weren't gonna be here today," said Seth, glaring at me. "Why'dja say that when you knew it wasn't true?"

"Well, I thought they'd said that," I snapped back. "Something must have come up. That's it. I'm sure that's why they were here today."

"I still think we should contact the sheriff," said Seth. "They're doing something bad. We could be in real danger."

"If we come back tonight," said Pete," when we know they're not gonna be there, it'll be a lot safer. We have to help Kate."

"We need those pictures in the phone, at the very least," I said. "Look, we'll be fine. I'll come by your place at midnight. My dad's asleep by then. What about your folks?"

"Our parents always go to bed at eleven," said Pete. "Midnight is good."

We had just finished eating dinner. I caught my dad looking at my arms. "How did you get all those scratches on you? You didn't fall again, did you?"

The phone rang the next moment. As soon as he answered, he put his hand over the receiver and whispered to me, "It's Mom."

"Thanks, Dad, I'll take it upstairs." Happy for the reprieve, I turned my body away from him and punched out my fists in front of me in a silent cheer. I ran up to my room.

The time difference made it difficult to call my mom while she was traveling through Europe. I was getting good practice texting her. But that was before I lost my phone.

"I miss you, Mom," I said, all choked up.

"I miss you too, darling," she said, giving me a few seconds to control my emotions.

I can't believe I got weepy when I talked to my mom. All those times how I wished she'd leave me alone. Well, I guess I got my wish. It took my parents' divorce for me to realize how much I loved and missed her. I missed my dad too. But since I'd been here this summer, nothing seemed right. Darn that Lily. I expected more of his time and affection. Surely never expected Lily to be here.

My mom was going on and on about her trip. She had

been sightseeing and shopping, and couldn't wait to show me what she bought.

"I can't wait either," I said, looking forward to some new clothes.

"We'll go together to Europe someday," she added. "You'll love it there."

I told her I'd like that, but didn't add that I hoped it was just with her and not that nerdy boyfriend of hers. She thanked me for sending her photos of my birthday party from my new phone. Of course she asked about my dad, but said nothing about Lily. She didn't have to. I knew she didn't like her. We said our good-byes, and I went back downstairs.

Dad was on the phone and seemed caught up in his conversation. I waved good night and turned my thoughts to what was going on at the cabin.

That night, I got into bed with my clothes on. I faked sleep when Dad checked in on me before going to bed. The hands on my clock slowly dragged close to midnight.

It was time!

Chapter 12

I peeked outside my door. The hallway was pitch black. It wasn't long before I heard my dad snoring. Something else my mom always complained about. It was loud.

I left my room, feeling along the wall with one hand. A small flashlight in my other hand guided me toward the staircase. There were ten steps. One, two three, I counted and on four a loud creak sounded. I froze in place and turned off the flashlight, expecting my dad's door to come flying open any moment. But it didn't. Then I remembered my dad was a sound sleeper. I continued down the stairs. I was in a sweat. I slipped out the door to my bike.

Not wanting to make any noise, I quietly walked my bike away from my cabin down the road.

Pete had said that they'd meet me outside their place. After about a minute, I hopped on and switched the headlight on. That plus the full moon gave me enough light to find my way. Still the sound of the crickets chirping kinda spooked me out. You'd think I'd been used to them by now. Maybe this wasn't such a great idea. Gathering my courage, I pedaled slowly down the road and breathed in the cool mountain air, which helped calm my nerves.

As I got closer to the twins' cabin, I got off my bike and switched off my headlight. I walked my bike the rest of the way guided by the smaller flashlight I had in my jacket pocket. Only Pete was outside waiting for me.

"Where's Seth," I asked.

"Seth fell asleep waiting, so I let him sleep. He didn't really want to go tonight. So it's just you and me. We should get going."

With my hand, I motioned for Pete to follow me. We didn't talk the whole way there.

Shortly before we reached the tree house, we hid our bikes behind some bushes near the road. Sticking close together, we crept along to the grounds and around the back.

I was walking in front of Pete. A screech owl hooted and Pete yelped.

"You okay?" I said, turning around. "It's only an owl. Gosh, your nerves are edgy."

"Yeah, I'm good to go," said Pete.

We reached the wall surrounding the cabin, and Pete lifted me up on his shoulders. I was amazed he could do it alone. Not only was he cute, but he was strong. I felt myself begin to giggle. With a lot of help from him, and a little help from the ivy on the other side of the wall, I climbed over and down. Pete came in through the gate I had opened.

Once inside the grounds, we searched the ivy where I had fallen earlier. We didn't see my phone. No matter how hard we searched we found nothing. The phone had to be in here. I was sure this was where I'd dropped it. My heart sank.

Suddenly I felt sick to my stomach. Someone had found my phone; there was no other explanation. Fear rippled through my body as I broke out in a sweat. "Let's go," I said.

It was a good thing I had Pete to hang on to because I was blinded by the tears running down my cheeks. We left through the small gate. Thank goodness it was dark so Pete couldn't see me crying. I felt so helpless. Now those men had my phone. They had *me*. My life was in that phone. Maybe the twins were right, maybe we should call the sheriff, proof or not.

A hissing sound got my attention. I stopped dead in my tracks. "Stop. I think I hear a snake," I whispered. I decided this was worth the risk of turning on the flashlight again. I aimed the beam at the road and scanned it.

"Where?" Pete said, turning around, checking the ground. "I don't see anything."

I tapped my finger to my lips. He must have seen me because he shut up fast.

Carefully, I looked around trying to see where the rattle sound was coming from. Then I saw ahead of me a timber rattlesnake. The second time I had ever seen one. A few more steps and we'd be on top of it. The last thing I wanted was for Pete to see how freaked out I was. Stay calm, Kate. Stay calm.

Even in the dark, the moonlight reflected the fear in Pete's pale face.

I kept the beam trained on the snake and began stepping

backward. "Just give it space," I whispered as I reached Pete. "It feels threatened now. We need to back away and be quiet. It's a *venomous timber rattler*. It won't bother us if we keep our distance and stay still and calm. There's a woodpile over there. I think it's headed for that. These snakes are really shy and elusive and prefer to eat rodents and insects rather than us. They're night stalkers. Also, it's cold out tonight, and they don't like the cold weather."

I followed the snake with my eyes as it slithered away from us toward the woodpile. "It stopped hissing," I said. "Let's wait a minute." I scanned the ground around us, listening to the rustle of the leaves the snake made. When I thought it was safe, I signaled with my hand for us to get going.

We both let out a huge sigh as we found our bikes and headed home.

"We could have been bitten and poisoned," said Pete. "We got lucky, but what a story to tell the kids back home. Seth would have freaked out. He hates snakes."

"I don't like snakes either. We still need light to check the bushes bright and early at the break of dawn. You with me? Remember, our pictures are in that phone."

Pete nodded, but even in the dark, I caught him doing a Seth eye roll. I led the way back to our cabins.

I snuck back inside and crept upstairs, climbing over the creaky step. By the time I got back into bed, I was shaking. How was I going to explain this to my dad? If I couldn't find my phone, I'd need to find a good excuse about how I lost it. I could hardly tell him about night bike rides and hissing snakes and crazy guys in trees.

This was the first time I ever got up before the sun. Gosh, I felt tired. But I had to find my phone. I was back on my bike headed toward the twins' cabin.

There was a heated argument going on between them. They didn't seem to know I was there.

"I didn't scream," said Pete. "You're only saying that."

"Yeah, if I didn't get up and shake you awake, Dad would have come running into our room."

"What's going on?" I asked. They looked startled to see me.

"It's not nice to sneak up on people," said Seth.

"I didn't, you were arguing and didn't see me ride up. What's up?"

"Pete had a snake dream last night. His screaming woke me up."

"You're afraid of spiders," said Pete.

"Well," said Seth, "I'm not afraid of electrical storms like you are."

"So what if they spook me. Like you never got spooked."

"Not like you," said Seth. "I never hid under the bed."

"Yeah, who's the one afraid of taking chances?"

"You should have woken me up last night," said Seth. "That was a sneaky thing to go without me. You just wanted to be alone with Kate."

"Baloney, you never wanted to go," said Pete. "I bet you were pretending to be asleep. And besides, you would have freaked out over the snake. You..."

"Hey, guys, knock it off. Geez. We need to go back to

the cabin," I said. "I thought it over every which way on the ride over. Pete, we probably just freaked ourselves out last night, that's all. I hope no one has my phone. It's in that bush, I'm sure of it." Or at least I was sure I didn't want to tell my dad it was missing without one last really good look. So, there was nothing else to do but go back again in daylight. I just had to find my phone.

"Seth doesn't want to go back there, Kate," said Pete. "Maybe he's right."

"And tell them what?" I said. "We still don't have any real evidence. At the least, we need the photos on the phone. C'mon, I need your help today. My dad's gonna kill me if I lost it. Let's hope no one else is there. Only us."

"Kate, this is getting too risky," Pete said.

"Yeah!" said Seth.

"Guys, it's only dangerous if we get caught, and we're not going to get caught. I have to find my phone. After that we need to get inside the cabin. That's where all the boxes are. We have to find out what's inside them. I promise that once we find something we'll go to the sheriff. I know we'll find something. I can feel it. We're really close. We can't stop now. Besides, Seth, you said you would if..."

"I know," continued Seth. "If you got my e-reader back. Boy, this is the last time I'll ever ask you for a favor. Okay, let's do it and get out of here."

"You'll boost me up. I'll use the ivy to help me climb down again. I'll let you in through the gate."

We headed out on our bikes. Upon reaching the cabin the guys helped me up. I climbed over and let them inside. We searched the bushes. Nothing.

"Twice is enough, Kate," said Seth. "It's not here. Let's go."

"Sorry, Kate," said Pete. "Maybe it's out on the road somewhere. We'll look real carefully when we head back."

"Look. Guys, it's real early, so why not check out the cabin since we're already here."

"There you go again," said Seth. "We said we'd wait until we knew for sure that they wouldn't be here. Let's go, Pete. This is too risky."

"It is early, Seth," said Pete. "Let's take a quick look around and see if we can gather some evidence. Then we won't have to come back here. I mean, Kate's right. We're already here."

"First we have to see if we can get inside," I said, grateful for Pete's support.

"This is crazy," said Seth. "And I'm crazy to go along with you guys."

We approached the cabin window. There was more sun now, and the glare on the glass was at such an angle that it was hard to see inside.

Seth checked the front door. It was locked. Pete and I walked around the cabin to check for another way to break in. The only other way was through the window, which was also locked.

The boys jiggled the window to see if they could force it open. But it only budged a few inches and no more.

"Let me see," I said, "if I can get my hand through and feel around inside."

So I slowly pushed my hand under the opening of the window. I didn't feel anything, but realized that I could slip more of my arm through. The latch was within reach. After I released the lock, I resisted the urge to cheer. Cat burglar Kate, at your service! I had a talent for this stuff. Maybe I should be a private eye when I grow up.

As I pulled my arm back out, the twins grabbed hold of the window and pushed it up for me to climb through first. Then I held it up for Pete and Seth. After Seth climbed through, the three of us stood still for a few moments, allowing our eyes to adjust to the dim light before looking around. It was completely empty. No boxes, no guns, no bullets. Just a bare room with wooden floors and a door to what looked like a closet.

"The boxes must be in the closet." But no sooner had I opened the door than Seth, standing next to me, slammed it shut.

He ran across the room and jumped up and down flailing his arms.

"What's wrong?" I said. "You look like you saw a ghost."

Pete doubled over with laughter. "I bet he saw a spider. He has arachnophobia."

"I hate spiders," said Seth. He shuddered and scratched his arms like he had them crawling all over him.

Pete took his shoe off. He stepped into the closet to get a better look at the big fuzzy spider. In one swift motion, he killed it with his shoe.

A clicking sound caught my attention. I looked over at Pete, who was looking down. "What the…" I heard him say as the floorboards beneath his feet rose upward and a light turned on.

Pete jumped backward, barreling into me so that we

fell in a heap on the floor. His shoe with the dead spider squashed on the bottom had landed near me, practically touching my face. I screeched and rolled away, jumping up fast. I don't like spiders either.

Then I shot my eyes over to the trapdoor. It looked like it had some kind of springs on the hinges. Pete must've triggered it with his shoe. The three of us crowded around the opening. A wooden ladder unfolded from inside.

I climbed down first, followed by Seth and then Pete. I stopped and turned around. "This is a lotta steps. How far down do you think it goes?"

Pete and Seth both shrugged.

Cautiously, we continued our descent down the ladder, stepping deeper and deeper into the emptiness below.

My feet finally landed on concrete. Seth came next with Pete the last to step down.

As soon as Pete stepped off the ladder, it swung back up.

And the trapdoor slammed shut above us.

Chapter 13

When that trapdoor slammed shut, I thought of a lid closing on a coffin. This caused a flashback to Seth swearing there were bodies in those trunks. My belly flip-flopped.

I quickly looked for a switch. Something that would open the trapdoor and lower the ladder.

"Hey, guys," I said, about to ask them to help when Seth darted past me to his brother. He put his arms around Pete's shoulders.

"What are we gonna do?" Pete had started gasping for air.

"Hey, take it easy," Seth said, "calm down. There's gotta be another way out."

"What's wrong?" I asked. The brotherly bickering was gone. Seth was dead serious. He held on to Pete and rubbed his back. This was even scarier than the trapdoor closing.

"He's having a panic attack," Seth said, not even looking at me. "He gets them. Okay, Pete, you know what to do. Concentrate on your breathing. Breathe in slowly, then breathe out slowly. We're gonna do eight counts. Here we go. Start taking slow breaths."

Pete looked up at Seth and me.

"I feel awful," he said, trembling and gulping for breath while grasping his chest.

"You need some fresh air," Seth said. "That should make you feel better."

Fresh air. Right. Pete looked awful, but we had to get going. "Yeah, let's find some evidence and get you out of here," I said with all the confidence I could muster. Funny, it calmed me down, trying to be calm for him. "C'mon, Pete. We're here for you."

The feel of his clammy hands made me wince when I pulled him up. His knees wobbled as he stood up, but he did make it to his feet. His shirt was soaked through and clung to his body. His skin was a scary gray.

I remembered a kid from my class who after playing outside had trouble breathing. We were told he had asthma. "Does Pete have asthma, Seth?"

"No, he panicked when the trapdoor slammed shut. This can happen to him when he feels closed in." Seth kept his arm around his brother. "Okay, Pete. Stay cool. It was only a mild attack."

We gave it a couple of minutes, hoping Pete would start feeling better.

Seth and I searched around and couldn't find anything to open the trapdoor. Even with the abundance of light from the lightbulbs strung high up on wires along the walls, we couldn't find a switch. Wooden floors supported tracks. No rail carts were on them. There was also a ventilation system. The air was cool and we had no trouble breathing. Except for Pete, of course, who still seemed to be struggling a bit for more oxygen.

There were some areas that appeared to be replete with a file cabinet that bore a large gold-plated lock, a solitary desk with a singular lamp, and charts on the surrounding walls. No boxes. I blinked at the enormity before me. Tears began to trickle down my cheeks. In the quiet I felt my heart thump.

The twins held back as I went ahead. I followed along the tracks, and after a few more steps entered a tunnel. In the semi-darkness sat a long line of rail carts. My fingers itched to examine them. My knees began to buckle. I called out, not sure whether to be excited or terrified.

I ran back to the twins. "I found a tunnel."

"How far down do you think the tunnel goes?" asked Seth. "We need to find a way out of here." He brushed past me and was about to start down, but I grabbed his arm.

"Hold up, Seth. There's more. That's probably where the boxes are." I pushed ahead of Seth and checked it out. "I found them," I yelled back. "You guys gotta see this. These must be some of the boxes I saw Nick unloading from the van."

"Wow!" said the twins. "Look at all those boxes."

"We may not have another chance here," I said. "Let's open the boxes now, see what's inside, and collect any evidence we can before we find a way out."

"Forget it," said Seth, "we have to get Pete out of here now. His breathing is labored. His life is more important than any of those crummy boxes. I don't care what's in 'em."

Pete drew a deep breath. "I'm feeling a lot better," he said. "Kate's right. We're here now. Let's just do it and grab any evidence we can find and get out of here. I'll be okay."

I hoped Pete was right. He sure looked pale. But Pete was as curious as I was. He knew there was something questionable in those boxes. I just knew it too. Besides, he would never get Seth to come back here again, and we both needed Seth's help.

"We are so breaking the law here," moaned Seth.

"Yeah," I answered, "but we might have good reason to do it. Besides, isn't that what we're here for? It's the only way we'll know what's inside. Does anyone have a penknife?"

"I'll use mine," said Seth, already cutting into one of the larger boxes. When he pulled the carton open, a medium-sized package tumbled out.

"Be careful with that knife," I said, but was too late.

Seth had already cut away the white paper covering. His knife had slit open the plastic bag inside, allowing a white powder to escape. "*OMG!* Looks like cocaine. Be careful," I said. "Don't let that stuff get on you. Step back. Try not to inhale it. Put that package back inside the box."

"This is not good, Kate. It's not good at all," said Seth.

"Geez, is this the real stuff?" asked Pete. "Wow, I've never seen it before except on TV and in the movies."

Pete was breathing heavily again. Even his walking was concerning me the way he staggered. We all paused, and then Seth said what we were probably all thinking—at least, I know I was: "In the movies they kill people over this stuff."

I felt like the wind got sucked out of me. It's one thing to spy and figure out what's going on and risk getting caught. It's another thing to risk getting *killed*.

I stopped myself from worrying about Pete. We had to move on.

"We're done," I announced. "Let's head back to the trapdoor. There must be a way to open it. But before we go give me a couple of those packages. I'll tuck them inside my pocket. We have our evidence." They didn't even argue. They jammed my pockets full till they bulged and then we set about trying to get out.

Again, we searched around, but couldn't find anything that even resembled a switch to let us out. No luck.

"Maybe there's a way out through the other rooms," Pete said.

"Come on," I said, leading the way.

Two other rooms were stacked with antique furniture that I recognized from the shop in Asheville. I ran to another room and saw what looked like a lab. A big scale sat on top of a table with a spatula next to it. A stool sat in front of it and plastic bags were on the table next to the scale. In another room were tables with no legs.

"Look," said Seth, pointing to another table, "these must be the missing legs. The plastic packages from the other room are stuffed inside them."

One of the rooms held only trunks like Lily's. Then I thought I recognized the trunk Lily bought. There's that dent again that looks like an arrow. But what is it doing here?

I went close and peered inside it. The trunk was filled

with lots of packages.

Seth's voice interrupted my thinking.

"Where's Pete?"

"Huh," I said. My mind still on the trunk.

We both looked around and then at each other and ran out of the room. Pete sat on the ground in the hall wiping sweat from his face with the back of his hand. "Boy, it's hot in here, guys."

I caught Seth's eye. It was cool in the tunnel, a lot cooler than outside. We gotta get Pete out of here.

"Seth and I will close up the boxes. You stay here, Pete. We're going to get to some fresh air. Quick, Seth," I said. "We'll take our evidence and get out of here fast. These guys are definitely smuggling some serious stuff. Now that we have our proof, we're outta here."

"You go on ahead and we'll follow," said Seth, helping Pete up.

I led us down the tunnel along the tracks.

"Hey, Kate. Why don't we ride in the rail carts? Pete's tired and we need to get out of here fast."

"Hold up, Seth. They'll make too much noise. We still need to listen out for those men."

"So what if they make noise. We're in danger. We could all get killed." Seth's voice was up an octave. I knew he was scared. But so was I. Pete too, I'm sure.

"But we still have to be careful. We need to walk as quietly as possible along the tracks. Let's keep going."

"I bet you knew they'd be here today," said Seth. "You just said that so we'd go along with you."

"Don't be paranoid. Of course I heard them say that."

Or at least I thought so. "Do you think I want to get caught? Really, Seth."

Seth didn't say anything. He seemed to be struggling to hold Pete up. It didn't look easy. Doesn't this tunnel ever end?

After walking for a while, Pete asked, "How much farther?"

"Hopefully we're getting close to the end of the tunnel. We need to keep moving," I said, trying to sound chipper.

We'd only walked a few more steps when Seth called out, "Hey, Kate, Pete isn't feeling too well."

I turned toward them and tripped, slamming my hand against the wall. Suddenly the lights went out and the rail carts started moving.

The twins screamed in unison.

Chapter 14

If I hadn't had my eyes wide open, I would have thought I was wearing a mask. It was pitch black inside the tunnel. I couldn't see anything. Even I felt a pinprick of panic. Poor Pete must be about to explode! "Hold on, I accidently hit some switches. Give me a sec." Slowly I got up, clinging to the wall. My hand fumbled around for the switch and flipped it back up. No light, but the rail carts screeched to a halt. Searching again, I felt another switch that turned the lights back on.

I hurried along the tracks to reach the twins. "Are you guys okay?"

Pete sat inside one of the carts. His face looked green. "Maybe if you kept your head down that would help," I said. "Take some deep breaths too." Please don't get sick. "We're gonna find a way out. We have to keep moving."

"We need to get him out of here," said Seth. "I've never seen him look so pale."

"Okay," I said, "we'll have to ride in the carts."

Seth sat with Pete in one cart. I sat ahead of them in

another. I found a switch along the wall and the train started up.

Suddenly I turned around. Pete was slumped over. I rubbed my brow and focused my attention completely on Pete. My god! I thought, There's Pete Stavens, one of my best friends, and he's in big trouble. All I had been thinking about was what I wanted. How selfish of me. How stupid.

Seth proceeded to breathe and count slowly, hoping Pete would copy his rhythm. Pete's breathing was calming down, and his color slowly returned.

"Let's pray the exit isn't too much farther," Seth said.

We continued down the tunnel where the tracks curved around. A ladder leaned against the wall up ahead. "Look," I said, pointing to the manhole cover on the ceiling above us. Beneath two of the rungs, a barely perceptual switch jutted out. I reached out and pressed it down.

The train jolted to a stop.

"Seth, let's climb up and try to yank that manhole cover free. Pete, you sit on the ladder and hold it steady." Seth went first up the ladder. I was right behind him, and supported him as he tried to jar it open. Due to our lack of strength we weren't able to budge it. *No way were we getting out this way.* We headed back down and told Pete the bad news. All the while wondering what was out there.

"Guys, we need to get going. Pete, you okay? C'mon," I said. "We should be nearing the end of the tunnel. We have to be close now."

Pete shrugged his shoulders. "Okay," he said in a deflated voice. "I can't wait to get some fresh air."

I started the train up again. Eventually the tracks ended

and the train screeched to a halt. A ramp appeared up ahead that led to a wooden door.

When the twins caught up with me, I whispered, "Look." I pointed. "That's probably another way to get in and out of this tunnel."

My finger zipped across my lips. We crept along the ramp to the door. I listened for any noise when Seth lunged past. I grabbed the belt loop on the back of his pants to stop him. "Wait," I whispered. "We don't know where it leads to."

"It's gotta lead to the outside," he said impatiently.

It took all my effort to open the door, which revealed a well-lit room crowded with antique furniture. Suddenly the sound of clomping footsteps shattered the silence.

Like rats, we scurried away. We jumped into the carts. I found a switch and slowly chugged through the tunnel. I kept checking back to see if anyone had followed us. No one followed.

After going a short distance, I stopped and said to the twins, "That must have been part of the restoration shop."

"What are we gonna do now Kate?" asked Seth. He turned to Pete. "You gonna be okay? Keep taking deep breaths. We'll find a way out."

I had no idea how to escape. I just knew we couldn't let them catch us. The thought of that petrified me. Yeah, big brave Kate was scared. We had to find a way out. The tracks ended and the train came to a stop. "We need to find something that will open the trapdoor and lower the ladder," I said.

Then the hollering started. The tunnel served as an

echo chamber. I could hear feet echo toward us. Only they weren't coming from the direction of the restoration shop. I recognized Max's voice and stopped dead in my tracks. The twins heard it too. We were trapped halfway between the trapdoor and the ladder, with a drug dealer…murderer between us.

Max screamed again. "Why are the lights on? Someone found the trapdoor. Case this place out fast!"

"Get Joe," I heard Max scream. "NOW! Someone's been in here." His voice sounded frantic.

"Guys, I see a switch. Let's turn off the lights," I whispered. "Maybe this will stall them a bit." Hugging the wall we kept moving back down the tunnel. I whispered, "Let's hide in one of the rooms."

As soon as the lights went off, I heard a heavy pounding on the steps, and a noise like someone falling. Another voice cursed. "I hurt my ankle." It was Max.

It was pitch black inside the tunnel. I kept moving and stayed close behind the twins.

"There's someone in here," yelled Nick. "I saw movement up ahead earlier. Stop," he yelled at the top of his lungs. He kept yelling for us to stop.

Was he crazy? No way would we stop.

"Help me out here and get those lights back on." It was Max's voice again.

Than what sounded like Joe's voice called out. "Found the switch," he yelled, and lights came back on.

Nick's voice reverberated down the tunnel. "Hurry up, Joe. They're up ahead. Stop them, Joe, stop them."

When I looked back, I got a sick feeling. Joe was closing

in on us. He might be fat, but boy was he fast.

We all stopped when we saw the ladder and the open manhole cover. Two men came down the ladder. We threw ourselves flat against the wall. The men headed in the direction of the restoration shop. They didn't see us, and by now the yelling had stopped.

"Hurry, guys. Get up the ladder fast." Seth helped Pete, who was gulping for air up the ladder.

"What if someone's out there, Kate?" asked Seth as he followed Pete up.

"Just pray there isn't," I said. "It's our only chance. Hurry, get going."

Pete and Seth climbed up and out through the open manhole. Seth called back down for me to hurry. "There's a lake out here and a stream. I see a canoe. It looks empty. C'mon, Kate, start climbing."

Seth reached back in and extended his arm down to me. I was up the ladder and grabbed hold of his hand when I missed a step and slipped. Someone had taken hold of my left foot. I looked down and saw Joe.

Holding on to the ladder with only one hand, I tried to kick him with my right foot, but he grabbed hold of it. Now Joe had both my legs. I screamed and tried to kick, but couldn't.

As I struggled for a way to free myself from Joe, I lost my grip on Seth's hand. Joe pulled me down the ladder. I held tightly to the rungs as Joe yanked me down. At the first chance I got, I let go with one hand, twisted around, and reached out for Joe's face and poked my fingers in his eyes. Something I'd learned in a safety course at school.

Joe howled and let go of my feet. He slid backward and caught his foot in the bottom rung as he fell off. The ladder swayed.

I scrambled back up the ladder. Seth grabbed hold of both my arms. My legs dangled in the air. But Seth had a strong hold. I heard him call out to Pete for help. Together, they pulled me up and out onto the grass.

I helped Seth push the manhole cover over the hole.

As I looked around, I got my bearings. Pete was on the ground breathing heavily. Gulping at the air around him. Ahead I could see a lake. We were in an isolated area that was unfamiliar to all of us.

We raced to the canoe, half carrying Pete. I nearly screamed with happiness when I spotted paddles in the bottom of the canoe.

By now the men had managed to get out and were chasing after us.

We got into the canoe, with Seth at the bow after pushing us off, and Pete in the middle seat. I sat behind Pete.

As we paddled barely perceptible curses rose from the shore.

Suddenly, Pete yelled, "Look! There are hills ahead of us."

"Slow down, Seth," I yelled.

We slowed the canoe down close to the shoreline and jumped out. I grabbed my paddle and called out to Seth and Pete. "Take your paddle in case we need them!"

As we ran for the hills we heard shouting behind us. Four men had run out from some kind of alcove in the hillside and were chasing after us. I remembered that Max had mentioned something about a cave. So this was what they had spoken about.

I ran past Pete waving my paddle. I noticed he was breathing heavily again. "They're with Max," I yelled.

Seth was ahead of me, but turned back to help his brother. "C'mon, we need to get up this hill."

I scaled the hill first. Our shoes got tangled at times in the weedy, rocky terrain, and it was tedious. Seth and Pete followed behind. They struggled with each step like I did. Seth stayed behind his brother, pushing him up. Too slow. Too slow!

I reached the top and looked down. The men were gaining on us. "Hurry," I called down to the twins.

As soon as Pete and Seth joined me, we found use for our paddles. We gathered rocks and threw them at the men below us. Then we rolled some larger ones down the hill. We pushed off as many rocks as we could. It seemed to be working. Whoever was below us hollered out to the others to take cover. I could hear screams and curses hurled our way.

I held up my paddle and yelled back at Seth, "Let's hold on to these." We turned around and raced away quickly.

No sooner had we started running than we heard Pete scream. Seth and I stopped running and looked back.

Pete was sprawled on the ground.

Chapter 15

Seth and I looked at each other. Pete was on the ground. We ran back to him, and that's when we noticed he had caught his foot in a gopher hole. What a time to fall, I thought.

"I think my ankle's broken," said Pete, through gritted teeth.

"Can you bear weight on it?" I asked, as we helped him up. A loud howl was his answer.

We caught him before he went down again, holding on to him tightly. His body shook all over.

"Maybe it's just sprained," I said. "Remember that summer when I sprained my ankle? It hurt real bad and swelled, but it wasn't broken."

"Yeah, maybe," said Pete, looking worried.

"I know it hurts, but we gotta keep moving. Those men were right behind us. Lean on us," I said. "We have to move more quickly."

Pete hopped as best he could on one foot, but the truth was Seth and I were practically carrying him at this point.

It was exhausting. Seth looked at me. I just nodded as if I felt the same way. We both knew we had to find a place to hide. And fast! But where. There didn't seem to be anything around us.

We dragged on some more when I spotted a stable. It looked familiar. "I know this stable," I yelled. "Seth, wait here with Pete. I'll run ahead to check it out."

When I approached I got a good whiff of the horses. The stable and the truck outside belonged to Hank. Rushing inside I not only smelled the horses, but saw my favorite.

"Hank, Hank," I yelled, over and over once inside. Two of the four stalls held horses. Racer, the one I'd ridden several times, occupied one. He turned my way when he heard my voice and poked his head out. Boy, did I miss Racer last summer. I ran over and gave him a big hug. His tail lifted upward, showing he was happy to see me. He remembered me after all this time. "Where's Hank, Racer?" I asked. As if he could answer. But by now I think I figured it out. Sure enough. I hadn't noticed there had been two cars outside when I rushed into the stable. Shoot! He was probably out giving a riding lesson.

I hurried back to the twins and helped Seth with Pete. Somehow he had managed to drag Pete closer to the stable. We both staggered in with him. He lowered Pete to a bench and sat down next to him.

"Hank should be coming back soon," I said, "but we can't wait. We need to take the horses and get away from here. Grab what you're used to riding. Let's get out of here."

Seth looked at me like I was crazy and didn't move.

"Hurry!" I barked. Then it hit me. "You don't know how

to ride, do you?" *Why did I assume they knew?*

As I thought that, I remembered when I first learned to ride. I was a pretty daring kid and couldn't wait to climb on top of a horse. That's where Hank came in. He and my dad were pals.

Hank had taught me to ride on Racer. I loved that horse. Something that day had clicked inside me. A new, even more daring Kate had emerged. I felt power sitting atop Racer. Hank had let me ride her whenever I came to the stable.

Seth's voice brought me out of my reverie.

"We've been on horses before, but no way can we ride fast. We don't know anything more than trotting. Besides, how can we get Pete on a horse in the first place without killing him? Look at the guy; he's in pain."

Pete was in pain. I knew Seth was right, but still. Those guys were coming! I thought for a moment. "Okay, I'll go for help. You hide with him up in the loft."

We leaned the ladder against the side of the loft. It was a struggle, but we got Pete up safely. We came close to falling off the ladder and exhausted ourselves doing it. It might've been easier if we'd lifted him up on a horse, but no time for regrets now. Every second counted. By the time we settled him on a pile of hay, his ankle had swelled.

When my breathing slowed down, Seth held on to the ladder while I climbed back down. I'd only taken two steps when a car door slammed shut outside.

"That must be Hank," I said and hurried down the ladder.

"Wait, let me look outside first," and he ran to the

window. "Oh no, it's Max and Joe," he cried out. "They're headed toward the stable."

"Quick! Help me off here." I reversed and proceeded to climb back up. I have to admit my body was trembling.

We tugged the ladder up to the loft and pulled it out of sight without a second to spare. We didn't dare make a sound.

"They weren't that far ahead of us," said Max from below. "They have to be close by. Let's case this place."

After a few minutes, Joe called out, "Nothing here, Max."

"Ditto here," Max said between sneezes. "Dang horses. See if you can find the ladder. We need to check above us," he wheezed.

Then something banged against the loft. Sounded like Joe found another ladder.

I'd noticed a pitchfork in the loft earlier. I held it up to Seth. "If Joe comes near the top," I whispered in his ear, "we'll use this to push him off. Then we'll pull the ladder up. I doubt there's another one."

"Good plan," whispered Seth.

Suddenly I saw rungs appear over the top of the loft. Seth and I stood together clutching the pitchfork. The ladder swayed from Joe's weight as he climbed up.

Seth and I were ready to attack him before he reached the top. Okay, I signaled with my fingers. On the count of three. One, and before I could show two, Max called out to Joe.

"Joe, Joe, forget the loft. Get down here," wheezed Max. "I need help. I'm having trouble breathing."

I yanked the pitchfork out of Seth's hands, away from the ladder. Poor Seth went flying backward. He landed on a high pile of hay.

"Hey, why'd you do that?" whispered Seth, looking confused.

"Joe's not climbing up. Max called him back. Max is wheezing something awful. Listen, you can hear him all the way up here. Something's wrong."

Joe hurried back down to Max. There was a crashing sound.

Seth and I peeked down. Joe was on the ground. He looked stunned, but seemed to recover quickly. He rushed over and knelt next to Max. Max's wheezing had worsened.

His voice sounded breathless.

As Max gasped for breath, he grabbed his throat. "I can't, I can't breathe... Asthma—have to get—out." He used Joe for a crutch and stumbled out of the stable gasping for breath.

We peeked over the ledge again. When they were out of the stable, we ran to the window and watched them drive away.

Seth fell to the floor and wiped sweat from his face. We turned back to Pete, who was lying there with his eyes closed, moaning softly.

"I'm going to ride for help now," I said, "but I'll use a password when I come back so you'll know it's safe to come down. I'll yell 'paddle.' We're going to be okay," and flashed him my confidence smile. "Hopefully Hank will get back before I return. Tell him to call the sheriff. Well, you know what to say. Okay?"

"Got it. Hurry, Kate. We need to get out of here. Pete's really hurting."

"First," I said, removing the packets from my pockets, "you keep these. Our evidence. Hide them. Also, keep the pitchfork close by." He looked almost funny, our book-worm standing there with a pitchfork in his hands. "Think you can use it?"

He looked me in the eye, unflinching. He didn't look so funny anymore. "They're not getting near my brother. I'll use it."

I had to go now. We lowered the ladder down. Seth held on tight as I climbed down.

When I landed, my knees felt wobbly. I looked up at the loft. My friends were up there. And it was my fault. I'd gotten us into this. I had to get us out.

I ran over to Racer and grabbed the English saddle I'd found earlier and put the bridle on him. But it took a couple of tries to mount him, I was so nervous. *Calm down, Kate,* I told myself. I took some deep breaths like Seth had Pete do. It worked.

I galloped down the road thinking I was safe till a car came behind me. Was that car following me? Goose bumps covered my arms. I didn't dare turn around. I galloped faster when I sensed the car was closing in. I turned in to a densely wooded area where a car couldn't follow. I found a wide tree that would conceal me. Think, Kate, think, I thought. But the next moment a familiar voice hollered out.

Nick's voice. Nick was close by.

"Max said she'd be around here someplace," he said.

"Let's spread out."

Nick and the others were headed my way looking for me in the woods.

"I hope I find the brats," someone growled. "I'll let them know what it feels like to have rocks thrown at your head."

I didn't recognize the voice. It must have been one of the men from the cave. My heart beat faster. I had circled so many times that I had no idea where I was right now. Great time to get lost, Kate! I knew I had to somehow stay hidden and wait. Afraid to even breathe, I repeated prayers over and over that they wouldn't find me. I made promises that I would never do anything bad again. I wouldn't give my dad a hard time. I'd keep my room neat, and I'd even be nice to Lily.

I had trouble keeping Racer still. The noise from the men talking and shouting disturbed him. Rubbing his withers helped to calm him down.

My mind raced. This was no game. We were in trouble if they found us. What am I gonna do? My head hurt from thinking so hard. The twins were right. As soon as I'd suspected these men were dangerous, I should have gone to the sheriff. But no, I had to handle it myself. Big shot Kate, acting like nothing ever bothers me. I hadn't done it on purpose, though. Never once did I think that this adventure would turn out like this. I tried to find some solace in that, but couldn't. I wanted this to be a bad dream and wake up safe in my bed, with Dad down the hall. But it wasn't. How could I have been so thoughtless? Why did I take so many risks? Seth was right. I was crazy. I thought of how I let the twins down. How they trusted me. I never felt so alone. I wished I could call my dad for help. But of course I had lost my cell phone.

What if Max had found it? My phone could be ringing in his pocket at this very moment. I should have been home by now. Maybe my dad had gone to the sheriff. What was he thinking? And the twins. Their parents must be frantic.

Meanwhile, the men's voices around me were trailing off. I continued rubbing Racer's withers to keep him calm. I whispered soothing words into his ear. Racer sensed something was wrong and remained quiet. Standing still like this, not making any noise, wasn't easy for him.

Then I made a decision. I couldn't let Seth and Pete down. The men couldn't hurt me if they couldn't catch me. I knew how to ride fast and with Racer's help, I could be back here in no time. Just get to the sheriff, Kate.

I crept along slowly on my horse till I was out of the woods and back on the road. It appeared the coast was clear, so I urged Racer forward. But I had headed due west, and the late afternoon sun was blinding me. I put up my hand to shield my eyes from the sun.

A figure in silhouette on horseback rode toward me. My name was called. I grinned broadly. I know that voice.

Chapter 16

"**K**ate! Thank god you're safe. We were worried about you. Where are the twins?"

The silhouette came closer into view. I was right, it was Lily. Never thought I'd say this, but I was glad to see her.

Wait—the twins…

How did Lily know they were with me? And—what was she doing here? She was supposed to be back in New York. When did she learn to ride like that? Why wasn't my dad with her?

An uneasy feeling crept over me. Although she was smiling as she rode toward me, there was something in her tone of voice that made me feel uncomfortable. My gut told me to back away from her.

Suddenly I heard Max behind me, yelling out, "Hey, boss" to Lily.

How was that possible? "Boss"? Lily was the boss? The voice in my head was back. Get away, Kate. Run!

Racer sensed trouble and twisted away just before Lily charged toward me. But she was amazingly fast. She rose from her horse and reached over and grabbed Racer's bridle. The fast-moving horses slammed together. Lily's horse reared, throwing her off his back.

Racer galloped away in time to steer clear of Max. Voices shouted from behind me. I glanced back. There was a group of men chasing after me in a truck. Everything I had learned about riding came into focus. Never would I have believed I could ride as fast as I was now. But Racer was going that extra mile for me. He was smart and sensed danger. Still it wasn't long before I heard hoof beats. I glanced behind me. *That can't be Lily.* But it was. Apparently she had gotten back on her horse and was out to get me. Boy, she had me fooled. I raced down the road. I grabbed on to Racer's mane and the wind whipped my face.

Up ahead I saw a trail and turned on to it. Racer was breathing heavily. I had no idea where this trail was leading me. It was too narrow for the truck to follow, but Lily was still there. It sounded like she was getting closer. The hoof beats were getting louder and louder. My only chance of shaking Lily was to get off this trail and back onto the road. At this point it didn't matter where I headed. As long as I got away.

"Faster, faster," I called out to Racer, letting up on the reins, pushing him forward. Racer sensed the urgency and galloped faster, breathing harder and harder. His hooves pummeled the ground. I worried they would crack from the trauma. At any moment the ground beneath me could explode. I had to keep going. But where?

I risked looking behind me and didn't see Lily. I had lost her. I eased up on my horse a little. The sun had started to set. It was blinding me. I struggled to see ahead. Where was I? For the first time secure in my saddle, I slowed Racer to a lope.

Someone suddenly grabbed my horse's bridle, and a powerful yank pulled me off. My world turned black.

I must have been unconscious a long time because once again I was in one of the carts inside the tunnel. I became aware of voices around me. They sounded like they were getting fainter, moving away maybe. Slowly everything started coming back to me. The last thing I remembered was being pulled off my horse. Now my head, wrists, and ankles hurt.

When the voices faded away, I opened my eyes. I tried to move my hands and feet but couldn't. They were bound with tight restraints that cut into my skin.

Footsteps. A familiar voice. "Well, sleeping beauty is finally awake." I looked up. Lily stared down at me. "You couldn't mind your own business, could you, kid?" Her voice so hard and mean that if I had my eyes closed, I'd never have known it was Lily. She walked away and returned a few minutes later with Max and Nick. The look on their faces made my blood run cold.

I shrank further down inside the cart. Max reached in and pulled me up with his bulging tattooed arms. "Where are your friends? Are you pretending to be alone?" he growled as he shook me violently. It's a wonder my teeth didn't fall out. "Who knows about this tunnel? WHO!" he screamed.

It didn't even hurt when he dropped me back down. My body felt numb. My head was spinning. Nausea stirred inside me. I almost gagged.

"How long have you kids know about this?" Max reached inside his pocket and removed my cell phone, shoving it in my face. *OMG,* he found my phone. "There are pictures in here, so don't tell me you kids didn't know about anything until today. Who exactly is with you?"

"They left without me." My voice trembled.

"We'll find them," said Lily, glaring at me as she stepped forward. "I sent some men out looking for them. Then we'll take care of all three of you. Before you go, Max, take her out of the cart and bring her up front."

Max scooped me up and carried me away from the carts. His sickening body odor almost made me barf. Although it hurt when he dropped me on the floor, at least I didn't have to smell him anymore. I refused to cry out and thought of my mom. Boy, she was right on about Lily. She was right not to trust her. Definitely something to be said about a woman's intuition.

"You guys get moving," Lily said. "I'll watch the brat. She won't be going anywhere."

"We're ready to load the carts," someone called out.

"Let's go, Nick," said Max.

Some men came out of another room carrying boxes that they loaded onto the carts. One of them hesitated and turned toward me. He had a killer look in his eyes and a bandage on his forehead. I bet that bandage was the result of the rocks we had hurled over the cliff.

"Okay," said one of the men, "looks like we got it

all. Let's go." They exited the tunnel via the ladder leaning against the wall. The bandaged one gave me another threatening look. That guy gave me the creeps. Chills ran through my body making me shiver.

The carts began to move along the track. After a while, the sound of the track noise stopped. The sudden quiet scared me. That and being alone with Lily. Or should I call her "The Boss."

Boy, she'd had everyone fooled. Me. My dad. No clue at all. But then I recalled the phone call I overheard that day before going into town. Lily was angry about a shipment being late. Silly me, I thought it was about books, and all the time it was about drugs. And the trunk I saw in the tunnel. It had to be the same one that Lily had purchased that day we went to Asheville. I mean, how many trunks would have an arrow dent like that? I bet that new antique shop was selling more than antiques. That day, Lily handed Joe a piece of paper when he carried the trunk away. She told him it was her address, but I doubt that now. That was a message passed on to him. Just like in spy flicks I'd watched. Something else bad guys do in movies: Kill the witnesses.

My stomach really flipped at that thought. I'd gotten the twins involved and now…

No. No. I couldn't think like that. I had to get out of this, get help for the boys. Think, Kate, think.

All this time Lily had been lying to my dad. No way would I allow myself to think my dad was involved in drugs. My mind was spinning trying to remember what else Lily had lied about. Clues that I never picked up on.

But then again why would I have even thought about it? I bet that was HER dad on the phone that day. And that expensive apartment on Fifth Avenue—had she bought that with drug money?

Lily seemed busy with paperwork. That gave me time to come up with a plan. It had to work.

"Lily, I need to use the bathroom," I pleaded, hoping I guessed right.

"Bathroom?" She laughed. "You think this is a hotel?"

"Please, I really need to go." Then I started crying and begging, "Please, please! I really have to go!" I doubled over as if in pain, crying and moaning while sneaking glances at Lily.

What's taking her so long? I knew enough about Lily to know she wouldn't want a smelly cart. "I can't hold it," I cried out.

Lily jumped up and took some tape and slapped it over my mouth. Then she untied my legs. I felt like giving her a big kick, but my knees at first weren't too coordinated. Plus my ankles felt sore and it wasn't part of my plan. I held my hands out to her.

"No way, you don't need your hands untied." She pushed me ahead of her. I watched as she pulled a switch which activated the ladder and trapdoor. "Make it fast, Kate."

It blew my mind that we had missed seeing that switch. I had trouble breathing with the tape on my mouth. Lily was behind me as I ascended the ladder. Seconds away from going through the trapdoor to the cabin, I doubled over and rolled my eyes, making gagging sounds. It sounded like I was suffocating.

"What the… Oh crap, no." Lily reached to pull the tape from my mouth. That hurt. With every bit of strength, I swung around and used my bound arms as a bat and struck her in the left temple. Then kicked at her with my leg. She swayed on the ladder and crashed to the floor below, her head made a sickening sound as it hit the cement floor.

Chapter 17

Oh my gosh—I killed Lily.
I had killed a person!

I suddenly totally related to Pete's panic attack. I felt my breath catch, like I couldn't get enough air in my lungs, and my mind shuttered in darkness as I squeezed my eyes tight, tight, tight.

What choice did I have? It was me or her. Her or Seth and Pete. It was self-defense. I had to do it and that was that. But first I had to get help. Lily's goons had to be stopped.

I forced my eyes open, but didn't look down at Lily. Seeing her brains splattered on the floor or anything would make me sick. The ties on my wrists hampered my attempt to open the door. I listened for any voices while I struggled to turn the handle leading into the cabin. Hurry, Kate. I was in a sweat when I bolted into the cabin. Slowly opening the door leading to the outside I saw Joe was in the treehouse, but his back was to me. The men must still be in the tunnel.

Without wasting another second, I fled out the gate. A familiar sound, a whinny, caught my ear. Racer was tethered to a tree across the way. How was I gonna get on him with my hands tied? Impossible, unless there was something sharp around to free my wrists of these ties.

My eyes surveyed the area and stopped at a fence with barbed wire. Working as quickly as I could, I ripped through the ropes, taking care not to cut my wrists. But I did! My wrists stung as the blood trickled down. I pressed down hard on them with the tail of my shirt. Within moments the bleeding stopped.

Someone had changed Racer's English saddle to a Western one. I'd outgrown Western a long time ago but climbed on anyway. I put my left foot in the stirrup and swung my right leg over.

I mounted him like my life depended on it, which it did. Adrenaline pumped through my veins. There I was, riding like a jockey with my butt off the saddle. Never would I have dared to gallop this fast or thought I could for that matter. But the thought of being pulled off my horse again fixed that. No one chased after me. They still didn't know that I had escaped. No ambulance siren, either.

I breathed easier when I passed the twins' cabin, my cabin, the library, and general store.

A little farther on, I spotted the sheriff's station. I slowed Racer down. His body felt hot and sweaty and he was breathing pretty heavy by now. It was the same for me.

I burst into the station, crying and trembling. I shouted out words that came out garbled. The deputy at the desk looked up and came around and sat me on a bench. He called out to someone, "I need a glass of water here. Hurry up! Now, young lady, what's this all about and what happened to your wrists?" He took my hands in his. "Bring some towels too," he called back. The bleeding had started again, and by now my wrists were a bloody mess.

"A man called Max and his men had tied me up. But I escaped from them. They're in this tunnel where I saw boxes filled with bags of drugs. And they're looking for my friends, who are hidden in a loft in a stable and need to be rescued." About to reach inside my jacket for the packet of white powder to show the sheriff, I realized I'd given them to Seth to hold. "There's furniture in this shop..." but before I could go on, I kept repeating, "Please help my friends, please." The officer turned away from me, then handed me the glass of water that someone had brought out. He scratched his head and motioned for the sheriff to come over when he got off the phone.

"What seems to be the trouble?" the sheriff asked as he walked toward me. I caught his concern when he looked at my wrists. I started crying.

"Okay, calm down now," said the sheriff. "Catch your breath and tell me what's going on."

I repeated my story. The sheriff nodded his head and started questioning me.

"Who tied you up? Where's this tunnel you're talking about, and your friends are hiding in a loft?"

"Yes, the loft is in a stable on Saxony Road, across the lake. My friends must still be hiding in the loft. Pete hurt his ankle. Really, you gotta hurry. They're in danger. The cabin is on Hunter Road. There's a trapdoor in the closet that lowers a ladder that leads to the tunnel. There are train tracks and rail carts. When I was captured I had blacked out. I woke up in one of the carts. My hands and feet were tied." I went on to tell him about my escape.

"Bo is gathering together some men now," said the sheriff. "Bo," he said to the guy who brought me the water, "call the posse, tell them to get moving. We'll let them know where we're headed from the road. These men sound dangerous. We have to move now." He turned back to me.

"Quick, Kate. Do you have a number I can call to notify your family?"

"My parents are divorced. I'm here with my dad. Here's his number." I handed it over to the sheriff. "Please hurry. The criminals might go back there."

A man's voice could be heard throughout the station frantically calling for help.

The sheriff suddenly swung around. "What's that racket about?" he asked. "Who's that man?"

"That's my dad," I cried, looking around. My eyes locked onto my dad's as he burst into the room. He ran over to me.

"Kate, thank god you're safe," he said, taking me into his arms. "Your wrists, Kate. What happened?"

"Dad, we have to help the twins. And Lily is not who she pretended to be. She appears to be the boss of a drug smuggling ring who are after us."

"What are you talking about. Lily is what? I knew something bad had happened," said Dad. "When I called your cell phone, a man with an accent answered. Then he hung up on me and here I am. But what's this about a drug ring and Lily? I need the sheriff. Sheriff, where's the sheriff?"

yelled my dad, looking around frantically.

Just then the sheriff returned, and I noticed the expression on his face had changed. "That was the Stavens, Kate. They just reported their boys missing."

Dad stepped closer. "What do the twins have to do with this? Please, someone fill me in. Kate, tell me what's happened."

"So you're Kate's dad. I just left a message on your phone to call me."

My voice trembled as I told my dad about discovering the tree house, cabin, and tunnel.

By now the station had swung into action. The mounted unit ran to saddle up their horses.

"Sheriff, my daughter said it's my friend's stable. I can lead you there."

"Okay," said the sheriff. "Kate, we'll need you to draw us a map where the cabin is. Can you do that?"

I nodded. Finally!

The sheriff's men took care of Racer. We rode out in police vehicles. An ambulance had been dispatched and followed after us.

I caught snippets of some of the radio transmissions. A road block had been set up. The sheriff showed his badge, and we got through.

We took a winding road around the lake. I spotted the hills. "That's it. Slow down. Those are the hills we climbed. That's where the stable is." I kept my fingers crossed that the twins would be safe and sound.

We continued around the road to Hank's stable. There were two people dismounting their horses.

"There's Hank," I said. He was leaning inside a car's open window, then stepped back and waved good-bye. My dad waved him over.

"Hey, pal, good to see you," said Hank. "Say, this is a sheriff's car. What the—what's a posse doing here?"

The sheriff got out of the car and came around to Hank. He immediately filled him in and told him to wait outside with my dad and me. Once they checked out the situation, we'd be allowed inside.

Guns drawn, the sheriff and his men went inside the stable. I gave him the password, and could hear him yelling "Paddle, paddle." Then he stepped outside.

Please, please, tell me the twins are okay. The sheriff shook his head and waved us in. My knees buckled at thinking something bad had happened to my friends.

"Kate, we yelled out paddle, but got no response. You give it a try."

I yelled, "Paddle, paddle!" before I even stepped inside the barn. "Seth, it's Kate!" I hollered "paddle, paddle" over and over. "Lower the ladder! Seth, Seth."

Seth looked down at me from the loft's ledge. "You did it!" The relieved look on his face made me cry.

"Lower the ladder, kid," said the sheriff, "so we can climb up and get you out of there."

Seth lowered the ladder to the ground with the help of the men below.

"Seth, we're safe, we're safe," I said, running over to him as he stepped off the ladder.

"Boy, am I glad to see you. I thought we'd never be rescued."

We hugged each other and watched the paramedics carefully lower Pete from the loft. He gave me a weak smile and I squeezed his hand.

"I heard someone calling, 'Paddle, paddle,'" said Seth, "but I didn't know who it was. Then you called out. Look, I promised Pete I'd ride to the hospital with him. He's in bad shape. Do my parents know about this? We've never been this late before. Can someone call them for us?"

"Your parents had called the station. You're right. They were worried about you guys," I said. "They're probably waiting for you at the hospital."

Seth rode ahead with Pete in the ambulance. Sirens and all. I bet they liked that. I would have.

My dad held on tight to me on the way to the hospital. My wrists and ankles were bruised and needed fresh bandages.

Pete was still a bit sleepy from the pain medication he'd been given, but he still managed a smile when my dad and I came into his room.

"You stay here, Kate," said my dad. He left to join Pete and Seth's parents in the waiting room, where they were meeting with the sheriff.

Seth came around from the other side of his brother's bed. He did a fist bump with me. Then I fist bumped Pete. He was so groggy, he had difficulty lifting his hand.

"I'm sorry I got you guys involved in this. I should have

listened to you and called the police earlier. I'm so happy you're both okay. I don't think I could have ever forgiven myself if something had happened to you." Seth and I hugged each other, and I squeezed Pete's hand, which was limp by now.

"I realize now how thoughtless I was, and inconsiderate. This was dangerous. I was so cocky. You could have died because of me. I'm so sorry. Please forgive me, although I don't feel I deserve it."

"Are you kidding?" Pete said, slurring his words. "Seth and I can't wait to tell the kids back home. Without you there wouldn't be a book."

Suddenly Seth noticed my bandages.

"We heard what happened to you. That must have been scary."

"I told you she was brave," said Pete. I just barely made out his words.

"Yeah," I said, "crazy brave. It was scary. Did they tell you? Lily was probably the boss of the smuggling ring? Can you believe that? Wait till you hear about it."

Sheriff Carter came into the room followed by my dad and the twins' parents. "We found your cell phone, Kate," the sheriff said. "Max had it on him. We'll need to keep it for evidence. We also found the tunnel leading to the restoration shop. No one was there, but Max and his men were found at the cave close to where you abandoned the canoe. This was quite an operation they had. Also, last I heard Lily's in surgery."

She wasn't dead. I hadn't killed anybody. Finally, I felt like I was fully breathing again.

The sheriff looked at the three of us. "You kids broke up a drug smuggling ring. These are dangerous people. We'll need statements from you for the record. We're very grateful to you. But I don't know if you really realize how lucky you got."

I nodded along with Seth. Pete was fighting to keep his eyes open.

"No more adventures like this," I said meekly.

"You could have been killed, Kate," my dad said. "If anything happened to you..." His voice broke off as he wrapped me in a bear hug.

I looked over at Pete. His parents were by his bedside with Seth and appeared weepy. They didn't say anything to me, but I could see it in their eyes that they blamed me for involving their boys. Or maybe it was me feeling so guilty for not notifying the police early on.

When the sheriff left, I told the twins that a reporter had called my dad. "He wants to come tomorrow to talk to us and get our picture. Remember when you asked, Pete, if this could make us famous? It just might!"

"Hold on, guys," said Seth with a twinkle in his eye now that all was well. "No reporters. We've got an adventure book to write."

The sheriff asked Seth to step outside so he could answer more questions. My dad followed, pausing for a second to give me a kiss on the forehead. "I'm so sorry, Kate," he said. "Everything was going on right under my nose and I never saw it. You tried to talk to me, but I brushed you off. I'll never do that again."

I threw my arms around him and hugged him as hard

as I could. When he went into the hall, it was just me and groggy Pete.

"Giving out hugs?" he asked. Then he seemed to realize what he said. His blush was the cutest shade of pink.

"Nope," I answered. "The hug was for my dad. This is for you." Then I leaned in close and kissed him on the cheek.

A couple of weeks later, the twins and I sat in the tree house.

Pete showed us the mock-up of the cover that he made for their book. Seth's first draft was gripping. Wow, that feminine hero was even braver and smarter. I wondered if my friends would recognize me. No matter. The three of us had an adventure of our lifetime. That's what really counted. What a writer. He made our adventure even more exciting than it was.

Seth sat there with the laptop on his lap talking about how he was going to email the manuscript to all the publishers in New York.

We joked about sending it to Lily. She'd suffered a concussion from her fall down the steps, and the surgery on her broken leg had been successful. She'd be laid up in a cast for a while—in prison. Maybe you should dedicate it to her," I suggested. That really got us laughing.

"Seriously, too bad you can't sign an e-reader," I said.

"No digital copy for my first book," interrupted Seth.

Pete cleared his throat loudly. "*Our* first book. This one will be a printed book. I can see it now. A novel by Seth and Pete Stavens." He eyed his brother. "Or Pete and Seth Stavens. Whatevs." Then he beamed broadly, as if their book was already in print.

I had no doubt that would happen.

CPSIA information can be obtained
at www.ICGtesting.com
Printed in the USA
LVHW091538161120
671823LV00038B/781